THE FURTHEST PALM:
The Trace Stories

THE FURTHEST PALM:

The Trace Stories

Rodger Jacobs

SILVER BIRCH PRESS

Los Angeles, California

Editor, *The Furthest Palm*: Lela Michael

ISBN-13: 978-0615682495

ISBN-10: 0615682499

Cover Photo: Brantley Aufill

Email: silverbirchpress@yahoo.com
Web: silverbirchpress.com

FIRST EDITION: 2012

"Hollywood Boulevard was a great screaming frenzy of cars; there were minor accidents at least once a minute; everybody was rushing off towards the furthest palm ... and beyond that was the desert and nothingness."

JACK KEROUAC, *On the Road*

Prologue

Woodrow believed that for art to have any everlasting value it must be challenging and unsettling and take time to absorb; for this reason he believed *Moby Dick* to be perhaps one of the greatest novels ever written and Edward Hopper the most masterful storyteller with oil on canvas ever. Woodrow found Hopper's desolately real urban and country settings, his painful attention to detail, to the hidden anguish and the dead vacant stares in the eyes of the occupants of his paintings, to be something almost heartbreaking to consume, whether in a gallery or museum or between the glossy pages of a coffee table art book.

When Woodrow first conceived *The Poet and the Pistolero* over coffee one fog-encased morning at a sidewalk snack shop in Venice Beach, an Edward Hopper image instantly came to mind. He would approach the painting as a European Romanticism window scene but with a twist: along with the outer view into the inner psychological scrutiny of the subject in the foreground, perhaps a young woman with a soft woolly head of hair in a drab gingham dress on a beige carpeted floor, the background action through the window just over her shoulder, with luminous shadows that reflected yellow light, would be the actual story he was telling with his artist's brush. That's where the drama with the poet and the pistolero would be playing out. He also noted to give the girl on the carpet a book or a magazine to apathetically leaf through while horrors are happening outside her window; with that notion he knew he had seized upon one of the key themes he wished to convey in the girl's face, that look of reserved ennui as important events happen behind your back.

Woodrow always sketched in charcoal before committing brush to canvas. Over the course of two weeks he feverishly rendered hundreds of samples of the girl's face, the room and the small bed in the corner with the white stone pitcher of water on the bland wood nightstand, and then the complicated segments, the violent, flame-fueled apocalypse occurring outside of her frame of reference. By the time he wore twenty charcoal pencils down to the nub Woodrow intuitively knew that the European Romanticism window scene was not the method to convey his drama. He lamentably returned his sketchpad to the top right desk drawer and determined to meditate on this momentary detour in bringing his tale to life.

The idea came to him one night while listening to NPR and drinking an affordable bottle of Pinot Grigio from Trader Joe's. Gone was the woolly-haired girl on the beige carpet. He would reverse the window scene, as Hopper had done in *New Haven and Hartford* and many other paintings, and reveal the outer view from an unknown interior perspective. The eyes of an unseen stranger cast upon the carnage.

It was time to open the tubes of paint.

The brush couldn't convey the paint to the canvas with enough haste and fury. Woodrow captured a fleeting glimpse of a railroad landscape as seen through a train window, introducing movement in the work. There was a track in the foreground that ran parallel at the bottom edge of the painting. The central figure was a tall man walking along the railroad tracks in his bare feet. He wore a slate gray suit that was shredded at the shoulder pads and thin wisps of smoke hissed from blood-soaked bullet holes in his white shirt, visible as the wind flapped the hem of his coat in a heavy breeze, evidenced further by the fine granular sand blowing around his naked feet. His eyes were cloaked behind dark glasses, symbolizing the hidden inner life that can only be hinted at in brushstrokes. Woodrow sometimes grieved that he had no talent for writing.

A railroad track in a desert in Mexico. No one peering upon the painting would ever know that Woodrow gave the man a name and a backstory. He chose the name Trace and discovered in his dog-eared dictionary that it served his subject well: a surviving mark, sign, or evidence of the existence of something that has long passed. A trace element. A bullet-riddled man in a combat-scarred suit walking barefoot along a railroad track in the Mexican desert. In one hand he clutches a book. A garish red cover and in black script the words COLLECTED POEMS can be discerned.

Trace, Woodrow's fantasy informed him, was a writer from L.A. who met a young, exuberant Hispanic poetess in a coffee shop in Los Feliz. God, she was beautiful, with eyes as dark and mysterious as Trace's own tainted soul. They became romantically involved and when the young woman – Woodrow named her Yolanda – was compelled to return to Mexico on suspicious "urgent family business," Trace doggedly pursued her across the border, learning to his horror that she was being married off to a low-level gangster to satisfy her father's extravagant gambling debts.

On Woodrow's canvas, at Trace's feet, her dark knees sinking in the sand, is Yolanda. The veil of her white wedding dress hovers behind her in the wind like a white flag of surrender. Her olive-skinned cheeks are wet with tears and she is pleading with him to go no further. On the other side of the railroad tracks there is a roadside taco stand and behind the taco stand bright magenta flames are dancing in the azure blue sky. A careful observer of the moment would note the vague outline of a handgun in Trace's waistband.

In the upper right hand corner of the canvas is a car engulfed in flames, a silver '57 Chevy Bel-Air, the driver hanging out the open door in deathly repose, mouth agape, frozen in mid-scream, a neat crimson bullet wound in his broad forehead.

"It's violent and it's surreal," the gallery owner said with a thin smile when Woodrow presented the painting for exhibition. "And it tells a story, doesn't it?"

"I guess so." Woodrow stuffed his hands in his pockets and scuffed the soles of his tennis shoes on the hardwood floor, eyes warily cast downward. He was uncomfortable discussing or analyzing his work.

"Don't worry, kid." The rotund man clapped a hand on Woodrow's thin shoulder. "It spins a good yarn with spare details, just like a Hopper painting. Isn't that what you were aiming for? Looks like it to me. Listen, people love a good tale in this town in any form they can get it, it's the whole creative inspiration thing, you see, movie people and all that, always looking for the next great idea, whether they get it from a painting they can stare at for hours or a late night lap dance at one of those strip clubs out by LAX. Not that I've ever been but that's another discussion. Empirical knowledge. I've got a lot of it. But like I said, don't worry. This beauty'll get your rent paid next month. It's good. It's garish in its own poetic way. That's what you were shooting at, right?"

"I wasn't shooting at anything," Woodrow mumbled. "I was just trying to tell a story."

ACT ONE:
January – June 2005

Darwin for Pigeons

"Did you make that pigeon blow up?" the little boy called up to Trace.

Trace was standing on the balcony of his fifth-floor floor residential hotel room. Moments before he was smoking a cigarette and observing the pigeons on the lawn below. There were two of the birds pecking and hunting for food. One was a slate-gray pigeon with ruffled feathers, a scruffy little fellow, and the other was a plump and stout bird. Every time the scruffy pigeon happened upon a scrap of something or other – pigeons will eat damn near anything, after all – the plump and stout bird would shoo him away and confiscate the morsel for himself.

Trace had a habit of tossing his spent cigarette butts over the hotel balcony railing and onto the well-tended lawn five stories below, relying on the moisture of the lush green grass to extinguish the burning embers. There were plenty of ashtrays in the room that doubled as his office and living quarters but once something became habit with Trace there was no reversing the course.

He finished the cigarette, took the butt between thumb and middle finger, and sent it soaring over the balcony. When the cigarette landed on the lawn the scruffy pigeon beat feet toward what it probably hoped would be something desirable.

"It's still lit, dummy," Trace muttered.

He turned his back to the balcony railing, anxious to return to work on his latest magazine deadline, when he heard a loud pop, like somebody imploding a small paper lunch bag. Looking down at the lawn, Trace saw what remained of the plump pigeon. The bird had simply exploded. The head and hindquarters occupied one slice of lawn and in the middle were the bright red entrails, flecked with the undigested remains of popcorn kernels, chunks of bread, what appeared to be a small dog turd, and, in the center of it all, a still smoldering cigarette butt.

"I didn't do it on purpose," Trace shouted over the railing to the small child who had paused on the sidewalk to observe the horrific scene. The scruffy pigeon was still at the scene of the crime, observing — perhaps in ironic wonder, if pigeons are capable of grasping irony and who is to say that they are not? — the fate of his bullying feeding mate.

"Go on now," Trace waved at the boy. "Don't hang around there. Pigeons are full of germs."

Trace wondered what to do next. Does one call Animal Control when a bird explodes? Or do you just leave the mess for nature to clean up? Furthermore, why would a burning cigarette cause a bird to explode like a feathered hand grenade?

He felt responsible for the gooey mess on the lawn below and the questions plagued him as he tried to finish writing his article about the exploitation of dead porn stars.

Two years prior, Trace had written a screenplay, *Claws*, about a flock of predatory condors that escape from the Los Angeles Zoo and prey upon the city's weak and vulnerable populace. During the process of researching the script he had become friends with Dewey Hopper, the chief ornithologist at the L.A. Zoo.

"A cigarette won't make a bird explode," Dewey laughed when Trace phoned him a half hour after the incident.

Dewey had encountered this phenomenon in relation to different types of birdseed, some of which contain types of grain that are unsuitable for different birds.

"It has to do with the size and speed of the bird's digestive system," Dewey explained to Trace, "and the amount the grain will expand when immersed in liquid."

It was more likely, Dewey said, that the pigeon had very recently ingested rice.

"If he had eaten a lot of rice and it expanded over a period of time, filling his stomach, well…you get the picture."

"Literally," Trace said, staring down at the mess on the lawn while speaking to Dewey. "Thanks, Dew."

Trace hung up, slipped the cell phone back into his leather hip holster, and lit a cigarette.

He wondered how pigeons survive in China.

To Protect and to Serve

"Fuck me," Trace hissed to himself. "It's the Lyndon La Rouche mob."

He tugged at the brim of his Rancho Vista baseball cap until it met his sunglasses and briskly pushed forward toward the green double glass doors of Border's Books on Brand Boulevard in Glendale.

Trace knew these jackals wouldn't respect his desire to escape unscathed. They could smell his attempt at anonymity and his apathy toward the cause of their crackpot leader. One of them – a tall, gangling man in shabby blue jeans and oversized T-shirt – leaped out of his rusted folding chair near the front door of the book store and made the error of intersecting with Trace's path.

"Sir, do you know what President Bush is doing to the Social Security system?" the man asked.

Trace stopped and pivoted on his heels until he was standing two feet away from the pamphleteer. He was probably in his late twenties. He had a long, unkempt brown beard and a head of equally unkempt and shaggy hair. Trace imagined that the bookshelves in the man's dark and sloppy apartment were probably littered with volumes on Marx and Engels and Che Guevara.

He probably likes Oliver Stone movies, Trace thought.

"Yeah, I know very well what the President's doing," Trace said, fishing a slender cigar out of his coat pocket and parking it in the corner of his mouth. He threw a glance at the folding table with neatly stacked pamphlets and fliers and a crudely hand-lettered sign that screamed DON'T LET PRESIDENT BUSH TAKE AWAY OUR SOCIAL SECURITY. The scrawl was downright child-like.

Why doesn't political activism attract calligraphers? Trace wondered.

"I can't sign your petition or whatever it is," Trace said.

Panic seemed to visit the man's face. "It's very important that we don't let the – "

"I can't sign it," Trace repeated. "I'm a journalist. I'm not allowed to align myself with political causes. It ruins my credibility, my objectivity."

"It's not like that any more," the La Rouche man persisted, "not with the Internet and bloggers and activism like that."

"I'm not a blogger. I'm a writer. I can't help you. Good luck."

Trace stepped around the shaggy-bearded man and entered the store, forgetting what he came there for. He left after quickly scanning the new releases and started back toward the hotel. As he passed the Bank of America, a petite Latina – obviously lost in troubles of her own – pounced through the exit and shrieked to no one in particular: "Son of a whore!"

Trace stopped at a bus bench and lit his cigar. He rifled through the canvas bag slung over his shoulder, rummaging through the groceries inside until he found his pocket notebook and scribbled the words down.

Son of a whore, he thought, I'll have to use that in a story someday.

As he reached the corner and hit the WALK button, a Glendale P.D. black-and-white glided to a stop at the curb. The young officer in the passenger seat shot a long, level gaze in Trace's direction.

Trace shifted the bag of groceries to his left hand, keeping his right hand free to carefully reach for his wallet, as he knew he would be asked to show identification.

"Where are you heading to?" the young officer demanded as he stepped out of the car. His left hand rested on the baton strapped to his leather belt with just a hint of malice. With buzz cut blonde hair and cold blue eyes Trace imagined the cop as a German tank commander emerging from his hatch in the African desert.

"Burger King across the street and then I'm heading home," Trace replied with as little tone as possible.

"Where's 'home'?"

"Pioneer Drive." Trace fished in his back pocket for his wallet and offered his I.D. before it was requested. The officer gave thanks with a curt nod of his head and strolled back to the patrol car to call Trace's CDL information in for outstanding wants and warrants.

"There's a reason we stopped you," the blonde officer said after dispatch confirmed that Trace was neither a wanted murderer, rapist, bank robber, pedophile, or anything equally unpleasant. The officer was suddenly unfolding a piece of paper in Trace's face.

"Does this guy look familiar to you?"

Trace was looking at a Xerox of a mug shot of a slate-eyed criminal.

"No. Never saw him in my life."

"You sure?"

"Yeah. What did – "

"He's someone we're looking for and I think he kind of looks like you."

Trace laughed. Actually he tried to laugh because right then he wasn't feeling very well. He bore absolutely no resemblance to the man in the photocopied mug shot but the tank commander begged to think otherwise.

"When did you get out?" the cop asked. His cold eyes took in every piece of Trace's wardrobe one at a time: the baseball cap, faded denim shirt with a ballpoint pen and a pack of cigarettes in the breast pocket, black jeans with a fashionable tear in the knee, old tennis shoes.

"Get out of what?"

"Did you get out of prison recently?"

"Um, no."

"Ever been in trouble?"

"Never been caught." A laugh choked in Trace's throat. The cop didn't think that was very funny.

"You have a job?"

"I'm self-employed."

"Oh, really?" He said it as if Trace had admitted to being one of L.A.'s thousands of street beggars. "What do you do?"

"I'm a writer."

"Uh, huh." Totally unimpressed. He studied the photocopy of the mug shot for a good thirty seconds and then rested his gaze back upon Trace's face.

"Are you sure this isn't you?"

"It's not me."

"Thank you."

The young officer stepped back into the cruiser. Trace hit the WALK button and waited to cross the street.

#

If that little twit doesn't stop stroking my drink cup like a phallus, Trace fumed, I'll be left with no other recourse than to pounce over the counter and dunk his acne-scarred face into the hot oil basket with the French fries.

Whenever Trace frequented any of the fast food joints within walking distance of the residential hotel where he lived – which was often, particularly when he reached the limit on his tab at the hotel restaurant – he always ordered the combo meals because they were cheaper. The problem was that he disliked sodas or any other carbonated beverage except for beer, which he probably consumed too much of, so he usually took an obligatory sip and then tossed the cup of syrupy goo into the trash.

That afternoon he ordered a chicken sandwich, sans the shredded green toilet paper they had the audacity to call lettuce, medium fries, and a medium drink. The kid who took his order filled the drink cup immediately, placed it on the counter, and then, while waiting for the rest of Trace's order, began having a friendly chitchat with one of his co-workers, all the while stroking Trace's drink cup up and down, up and down, up and down.

What's the deal, kid? Trace thought. If your buddy turns you on that much why don't you take it to the men's room and leave my fucking drink cup out of it?

It didn't matter that Trace was going to ditch the cup into the big orange trash container by the front door. What mattered was that Trace had to touch the cup. There was no area of the beverage container that the little prick hadn't fondled.

He watched the kid with mounting anger.

You are one stroke away, he tried to communicate wordlessly, from being a human with a French fried face. Or is that Freedom Fried Face? What the fuck.

The goddamn ghouls of 9/11 and their Orwellian Speak pissed him off and this kid behind the counter, this burger jockey who probably never read a book in his life save for whatever was required reading in high school, was the reason they were getting away with wars and rumors of wars.

"Do you want ketchup?" the kid asked in a monotone as he slid the bag with Trace's lunch across the counter.

"No."

Trace slid the paper bag into the canvas bag over his shoulder, fitting it comfortably between the bottle of Chardonnay and a few other grocery items he'd purchased at the market and gingerly took the soda cup between his thumb and middle finger.

He tossed the soda cup in the trash bin on his way out the door.

I've got to start eating better, he thought.

Trace and the Munchkins

Trace had a bad habit of tripping over little people. At six-foot-one, he simply didn't notice them at his feet until he was already stumbling all over them.

"L.A. is rotten with dwarves," Trace explained to Josephine as they lay in bed one night. "It's because of *The Wizard of Oz*."

Jo threw back her head and laughed long and hard. Trace impatiently waited for her laughter to subside before continuing.

"It's true!" he barked, lighting a cigarette and stumbling out of bed to open the balcony door. "When they shot *The Wizard of Oz* at MGM in 1939, the talent agents recruited midgets from all over the country to appear as Munchkins. Once they got a taste of Southern California life, a lot of them stayed on permanently."

"I can't think of a better place to be a midget than L.A.," Josephine said with another peal of laughter.

"You mock," said Trace, "but it's true."

The first time Trace tripped over a midget was at the K-Mart in Burbank while shopping with Josephine. It was 1999. Trace and Jo had been kicked out of their homes by their spouses after a Valentine's Day weekend tryst in San Francisco. After settling into a temporary hotel room, the shopping excursion to K-Mart was their first opportunity to stock up on much-needed supplies. Jo had lost everything, her husband assured her, all of her personal possessions, including her two dogs.

Trace and Josephine had gone their separate ways in the store. Trace picked out a new necktie, two Walter Mosley paperbacks, and a pair of black jeans. He trudged to the women's wear department of the K-Mart where Jo told him he would be able to locate her when he was through shopping.

Traversing the tightly packed floor of women's wear with the circular racks of dresses dragging the floor, Trace suddenly felt something small and very solid slam into his left knee. He jumped back, the Mosley novels flying from his hands and crashing onto the threadbare blue-carpeted floor only before bouncing off an object about three feet tall.

When Trace looked down a kindly looking midget was looking back up at him, rubbing a spot on the crown of his head where the edges of the Mosley books had struck him. Trace was also stepping on the small man's foot.

"Oh, Jesus, I am so sorry," Trace muttered.

"It's alright," the little man said and quietly moved on.

Another incident occurred at the residential hotel Trace and Jo now called home. Maurice Richard was a three-foot-five dwarf who made a decent living as a background and atmosphere performer in movies and TV. The first time Trace unintentionally assaulted Maurice was when he was picking up his mail at the front desk. He simply didn't see the little actor standing at knee level and when he pivoted on his feet to turn away from the desk, Maurice made direct contact with Trace's knee.

"Oh, Jesus, I am so sorry," Trace muttered again. He didn't know what else to say when he so violated the low air space of a midget.

The first incident with Maurice wasn't to be the last, however, and the two men learned to avoid each other in the hotel's lobby, restaurant, and serpentine hallways. Trace was certain that Maurice understood that he had no malice toward little people. He just didn't see them down there.

There was a stinging rebuke for Trace's unintentional assaults on little people and the moment was burned into his brain as if seared into the soft flesh of the cerebellum with a branding iron.

Trace was having lunch with an old friend – a TV news cameraman – at a diner on Olive Avenue in Burbank, not far from the NBC Studios.

"Check it out," said his friend, pointing out the plate glass windows to a small cluster of offices across the street. "The Billy Barty Foundation is over there."

"What do they do?" Trace mused. "Advance the cause of little people?"

"That, and offer self-defense courses in case they ever run into the likes of you," Trace's friend joked.

It had only been two weeks since Trace and Josephine began their romance. Trace and Gina were already discussing the impending divorce.

"Isn't that your wife's car?" the cameraman asked, pointing out the window again.

A white Toyota glided to the curb across the street and Trace's eyes followed as his wife emerged from the car and she walked into an office next door to the Billy Barty Foundation.

"That's a lawyer's office," Trace's friend offered. "A family law specialist."

Trace felt his heart drop into his groin. He didn't have the money to pursue a divorce. He had thought that he and Gina would simply talk about it until it became a financially feasible thing to do.

Over the next five weeks, as Gina's lawyer and Trace's paralegal hammered out the details of the divorce, Trace was compelled to drive to the lawyer's office to sign a never-ending series of legal documents.

And every time he briskly strolled past the front door of the Billy Barty Foundation to arrive at the lawyer's office he hoped and prayed that he wouldn't accidentally lay some poor midget flat on the hot Burbank sidewalk.

Satori

Two months had passed since Trace had a paying gig so when an aging and downtrodden gay hustler asked him to broker a deal with *The National Tattler* he swallowed his distaste for tabloids and agreed to meet the man.

"Our mutual friend tells me that if anyone can sell a story it's you," David Dulce said in greeting when they hooked up at a crappy sushi bar in Studio City. Trace hated sushi and since the joint didn't serve tempura or teriyaki he would have been shit out of luck if not for the saki to satiate him.

"You know what the Japanese say?" Trace asked when they settled in at a table near the rear parking lot entrance. "You can never have enough saki."

"Really?" Dulce studied him through cat-like eyes from a face ravaged by too many attempts at reconstructive surgery. "I've been to Japan three times and I never heard that one."

"What do I know?" Trace muttered, pouring his first shot of the hot fermented rice beverage. "Let's get down to it. What do you have to sell? You seemed kind of vague on the phone."

"Ten years ago I had an affair with – " He named a pop music superstar that everyone suspected was gay.

Trace didn't even blink. He poured another shot of saki, knocked it back, and wiped his mouth with the back of his hand.

"How much money are you looking for?"

"Well, Trace, that's the thing." He had a way of elongating his words that annoyed Trace to no end. When he spoke Trace's name it came out as a long train named Traaaaaaaaace. "I'm really in a bad place right now. I had to have surgery to remove a bullet that's been near the base of my spine for a long time."

"How did that happen?"

"Someone shot me the day after I got out of the Federal witness protection program."

Again Trace didn't blanch. Characters like David Dulce floated in and out of Trace's life with alarming frequency – alarming to those around him.

"What were you doing in the witness protection program?"

"I turned state's evidence against an Israeli Mafia guy in a murder case."

Trace was beginning to feel the saki's warm embrace.

"You have to set a price, David. How much do you want for your story?"

"Five grand?"

Trace laughed. "If your story checks out, David, *The Tattler* is going to offer more than five thousand dollars. Five grand is the beginning. That's my finder's fee."

David's feline eyes lit up like he'd just been cruised by David Hasselhoff.

"If it checks out," Trace underscored. "Are you willing to take a lie detector test?"

"Of course. I'm not lying, Trace." Traaaaaaaaaaace. Like a bleating sheep.

"Of course you're not."

That evening Trace called anti-porn crusader Duke Sebastian. Duke was remarkably well connected in the Hollywood underground and financed his anti-smut campaign by dropping a dime to the tabloids every now and then. He was even able to verify secondhand that David Dulce's story about his gay affair with the pop superstar was on the money.

Once Trace contacted the editor at *The Tattler* that Duke referred him to, events picked up at an astonishing speed. *The Tattler* flew a reporter to L.A. overnight to meet with Dulce. David passed not one but two polygraph tests with flying colors. He was either incapable of telling a lie or was a pathological liar who believed his own bullshit. Either way, *The Tattler* was buying the story.

The finder's fee of five thousand dollars was the end of a long drought for Trace but it wasn't the end of his relationship with David Dulce. *The Tattler* paid Dulce ten grand for his story but the aging hustler was so deep in debt that they may as well have offered him a thin dime.

Dulce began phoning Trace on a regular basis, urging Trace to sell more of his sordid sexual adventures to the tabloids. He offered a laundry list of sexual oddities that stunned even Trace: celebrity bestiality romps, three-ways, rape, who's gay and who is a diesel dyke, and who has the largest collection of kiddie porn on the West Coast.

"You're buying yourself a ticket to your own funeral with these stories," Trace cautioned. "And be careful about the messages you leave on my voice mail. The hotel housekeeper accidentally overheard that message about Siegfried and Roy yesterday."

In the long run, though, Trace couldn't interest *The Tattler* in any further David Dulce stories. For starters, the tabloid was going through an "editorial restructuring" and the editors left standing after the bloodletting looked upon David Dulce as a fringe celebrity at best. His greed was also apparent and nothing chills the blood of a tabloid editor like a gold digger – unless their price is reasonable.

"I'm sorry, David, I can't sell anything for you," Trace apologized for the tenth time in a week. Dulce was calling him every day, breathing dirty tales of dirty celebrities into Trace's voice mail.

"Come on, Traaaaaaaaaace. What about my Loretta Lynn story? Can't you sell that? It's hot!"

Trace hung up the phone and then dialed the four-digit extension for the hotel switchboard.

"I need you to screen all of my calls for the next month or so, please," he requested. "If a guy named David Dulce calls do not put him through. Tell him I'm on the other line, tell him I checked out of the hotel, tell him I died. I don't care what you say, just don't put his calls through, please."

Trace lit a cigarette and laid down on the bed, staring at the ceiling and pondering the bizarre story David told him about Engelbert Humperdinck.

Carver's Dog

Trace hit the hotel bar early that night. He was there at six o'clock sharp when José opened the double doors to the windowless den with a frayed pool table, a jukebox stocked with rock classics, and uncomfortable chocolate brown vinyl booths on either side of the room.

Trace poured his weary frame onto a stool at the bar and ordered a tall bourbon and water. His mood was as shaky and delicate as a fault line. Earlier in the day, his editor had bumped his two front-page features to the next issue, which meant he had to make a quick duck into the porno ghetto in order to pay the rent on his room that month.

"Would you like to write an all-girl strap-on movie?" his friend Norman, the porn director, asked when Trace called pleading for work. "Not a lot of story but enough to make a cable sale."

"Give me a few hours to think about it," Trace had said.

Thirty minutes later he called Norman back.

"We'll do a spoof of Chuck Palahniuk's *Fight Club* called *Strap-On Club*," Trace offered.

"You mean the movie *Fight Club*?" Norman replied.

"The movie, the book, whatever, the idea remains the same. A secret club to help vent frustration but in this case it's chicks instead of guys and instead of fighting they screw each other with strap-ons."

Trace's left ear, always prone to infection, throbbed at the violent burst of laughter coming through the phone receiver.

"That's a terrific idea!" Norman enthused. "Go write it up and I'll have a check for you on Monday."

Three hours later, with the script complete and delivered, Trace sat in the hotel bar nursing his third bourbon and water, trying to chase the *Strap-On Club* dialogue out of his head.

> TAYLOR BOURBON: I want you to fuck me as hard as you can.
>
> SUSAN: What? In your ass?
>
> TAYLOR BOURBON: Surprise me.
>
> SUSAN: This is so fucking stupid.

By the time he asked José for a sixth bourbon and water, *Strap-On Club* had receded to the back of his mind.

And then the dog appeared. As usual, Trace smelled the dog before he saw it. The animal was so old and decrepit that Trace couldn't determine the mongrel's age but clearly it was a very aged hound. Its brown and black coat had huge patches of fur missing and the exposed skin was red and scaly. The dog's black eyes were wet and glassy. Its left leg was game and its back was contorted in a painful arthritic hump. A tongue hung loose from the animal's moist, saliva-strewn mouth as if it were trying to escape the two rows of rotting teeth. And the smell of the animal was simply ungodly.

The dog's owner, by contrast, was a clean-cut, barrel-chested man in his late fifties. With the dog's leash firmly wrapped around his left hand, the dog owner occupied a stool next to Trace and ordered a beer. The two men exchanged a curt nod.

"What's the deal with your dog?" Trace blurted.

"How's that?"

"I can tell when you and your dog have been in the elevator be-cause the smell lingers for an hour."

The man drank his longneck Budweiser straight from the bottle.

"The dog's old and sick," the man said blankly.

"How old is he?"

The man hiked his shoulders. "Don't know. He was a pup when I got him in '88 but he might have already been a year old then."

"What's his name?"

"Bath."

Trace laughed. "Isn't that ironic?"

"How's that?"

"You never bathe the damn thing."

"Can't. He's in too much pain. Can't touch the poor thing really."

"Cancer?"

"Don't know, can't really afford to take him to the vet."

Trace then felt bad for both the dog and its owner. The man spoke again after another pull off the beer bottle.

"Not exactly ironic in the literal sense of the word."

Trace hated having his talent with words challenged.

"Well, sure it is," he said. "When you got the dog, I'm sure you didn't think the day would come he'd be so sick and decayed you couldn't bathe him. Hence, the name Bath is very ironic, I would say."

The man ordered another beer and contemplated Trace's words for a moment.

"I named him Bath after a Raymond Carver short story called 'Bath.' I got Bath in Port Angeles, Washington, in 1988 right after Carver died. That's where he lived, you know, Port Angeles."

"Uh, huh." Trace signaled José for a refill.

"I was doing yard hauling for a guy who lived down the street from Carver. He got three dogs from Carver's dog's litter and he said I could have one if I cut my rate just a little bit as he was on a limited income."

"Wow." Trace regarded the pile of leashed mange on the floor with new respect. "Raymond Carver's dog, huh?"

"Yup."

"But why Bath?"

"It's my favorite Carver story. You know his stuff?"

"Absolutely."

"'Bath' is the story about the mother who orders a birthday cake for her little boy but on the way to school on the morning of his birthday party the boy is hit by a car and – "

"Yeah, yeah," Trace interjected. "I remember that one. Altman used it in *Short Cuts*."

Two Union Pacific railroad workers swaggered into the bar. One of them fed a dollar into the jukebox and punched up 'L.A.

Woman.' Trace knew the two men. They would shoot pool and play Doors songs all night long.

"Well, goodnight," he said to the dog owner as he slipped off the barstool.

Back in his room, Trace searched his bookshelves for the Carver volume. There were books everywhere in his room. In the entranceway there was a bricks-and-board shelf laden with books. One of those Office Depot particleboard bookshelves stood next to his bed. More books were piled behind the ratty sofa and even more rested in boxes in the closet.

After an hour of searching he finally located the dog-eared paperback of Carver's *What We Talk About When We Talk About Love*. He stretched his legs out on the bed – they were throbbing from the psoriatic arthritis – and lay down on his back with the Carver book in hand.

Instead of reading, though, Trace fell asleep and he dreamed about naked women with large strap-on dildos being chased by an insane and rabid dog.

Trace Goes Mountaineering

Trace grabbed the hand strap of the rental car with white knuckles and braced for the hard curve in the road ahead.

"For fuck sake, slow down." he growled. "I have a problem with mountain roads."

His lead-footed wife, Gina, took her eyes off the road, which further terrified Trace, to throw a quizzical look in his direction.

"I'll tell you about it when we get to the hotel. In the meantime, watch your speed on the curves, okay? Shit."

They were traveling the eastern slope of the jagged Rocky Mountains towards Estes Park and the famed Stanley Hotel, the inspiration for the Overlook Hotel in Stephen King's *The Shining*. An hour earlier, Trace found himself in the office of the assistant editor of *The Denver Post*, engaging in a disastrous interview for a staff writer position.

The guy can see I'm not a team player, Trace thought as he squirmed in a chair, and my clip file is for shit except for the investigative piece for *Hustler*. Too bad the illustration next to my by-line is of a girl barfing with a cock in her throat.

"The *Hustler* article did me in with the *Post*," Trace told Gina. His eyes were clamped shut because she still refused to yield to his request for a reduction in speed on the mountain pass.

"I told you not to show it," she hummed in a self-satisfied tone. "You don't have the credentials to work for a newspaper yet."

The year was 1994 and Trace's credentials at that time were indeed limited to "leftist rags" and porn magazines. He made a living at it, to be sure, but Gina was always reminding him that he was wallowing in a ghetto. Gina was his first wife, the mother of his only child, and a demon spawn with the bitter taste of Failed Actress in her mouth. They were visiting Colorado for one week and the only reason Trace interviewed for the staff reporter gig was that he wanted to escape L.A.

When they pulled into the parking lot of the Stanley Hotel, Trace bolted from the Toyota Celica like a man fleeing his own execution. He lit a Marlboro with quaking hands and took in the odd white-pillared Georgian architecture of the hotel. It didn't look anywhere near as foreboding as the hotel in either King's novel or Kubrick's movie.

"Here's what happened," Trace said when Gina stepped out of the car. "In 1972, my mom married a guy, Bobby Tompkins, who had just finished two tours of duty in Vietnam. Bobby suffered from post-traumatic stress syndrome and was prone to violent passive-aggressive mood swings."

"Be careful not to smoke too much up here," Gina interrupted. "The air is very thin."

"I thought it was drinking you were supposed to be moderate about in high climates." He took a long drag on his cigarette and continued. "Bobby was a raging alcoholic to boot. My mom convinced him to re-up in the Army – the wrong tonic for a man still dealing with the stress of war but mom always was selfish in that way – and after two brief stints at Ford Ord in Carmel and Fort Dix in New Jersey, we were shipped off to Germany.

"We were stationed at Munich. Bobby had a friend from the war who lived south of us in Bad Tolz, Austria. We had to drive through some pretty dramatic and vertical mountains to get to Bad

Tolz to see Bobby's friend and his wife once a month. And wouldn't you know it, on the drive home through those winding mountains, with Bobby drunk behind the wheel of our station wagon, that's when my mom would start a fight with Bobby about his drinking. Bobby's answer was to punch the accelerator and scream, 'Shut up! Shut the fuck up!' as we careened around those mountain bends at sixty, seventy, sometimes seventy-five miles per hour."

Trace stamped out his cigarette in the gravel of the parking lot and threw up his hands.

"And that's it. That's the story. Ever since that day I've been freaked about driving in mountains."

Gina stared at him for a beat.

"You were thirteen years old, for crying out loud. You should have gotten over it by now," she said. "Are we going in the hotel for a drink or what?"

Never again could Trace feel a moment of tenderness toward her.

Bogart Sleeps Here

"But I don't write poetry!" Trace protested.

Marcel lit a cigarette and smiled at Trace through a curl of smoke.

"That's the theme of the next issue. If you want in, you have to contribute a poem."

"Shit."

The only reason Trace contributed anything at all to *Kidnap* was to expand his portfolio. *Kidnap's* detractors – and they were legion – dismissed the monthly arts and culture magazine as "a leftist rag." Marcel DuPont, the founder and editor, ran the publication out of a huge, dark loft that also doubled as his apartment near the Long Beach Harbor.

Marcel loved to shock. The issue that carried Trace's famed Jack London essay featured a gaudy cover illustration of Mary Magdalene giving Jesus Christ a blowjob. Marcel frequently published the rantings of anarchists, neo-Nazis, and extreme environmental activists, the sort that chain themselves to redwoods in an effort to halt deforestation. Trace had no desire to be mixed in with such a lunatic fringe but a clip was a clip.

"How much time do I have?" Trace asked.

Marcel laughed. "You speak as if I have pronounced a death sentence."

"Death sentence. Poetry. Same fucking difference."

Trace left the office in a mood as cold and gray as the drab industrial warehouses that dotted the harbor landscape. Marcel wasn't paying much, as usual, but Trace needed new brakes for his '48 Packard and any contribution to that fund was welcome.

Trace bought the 1948 Packard Touring Sedan, a California original, from an auto restorer in Eldorado, California. The car sorely needed some nice cosmetics, such as paint, but the body was solid and it drove smooth. The aggressive soccer moms in their monster SUVs had nothing on Trace when he was behind the wheel of his Packard.

He needed a drink so he pushed the Packard harder than usual, bobbing and weaving in and out of traffic as he traversed the ribbons of freeway that took him from the God awful bowels of Long Beach back home to the residential hotel in Glendale, eight miles north of downtown Los Angeles. Trace had a view of the L.A. skyline from his fifth-floor balcony and that was often his meditative focal point when the words weren't flowing.

"A poem," Trace hissed that evening, drink in hand, cold blue eyes fixed on the skyscrapers that jutted out of the earth and into the gray, sodium-flavored sky.

"All fall down someday," Trace said to the skyline. Speaking to inanimate objects was just one of his many quirks that annoyed most of the women who had floated in and out of his life. Trace was a monogamous creature prone to long-term relationships and it frequently mystified him that none of his former girlfriends expressed a desire to stay in communication with him after they split.

"You're a dynamic force," a holistic healer once told him. "The women who are drawn to you crave all of your attention or none at all."

"Whatever," was Trace's reply.

Trace had good reason to be intimidated by the prospect of writing a poem. The only poet he liked was Robert Service. The only thing he understood about the mechanics of poetry was iambic pentameter. Poetry was an alien language to him.

He played with words and themes for days. He parked words on paper and moved them around this way and that but nothing that spat out of his brain resembled poetry. He refused to read poems for inspiration because if he was going to compose one of the goddamn things it would be on his own terms.

The afternoon before his deadline he took the Packard out for a drive. He drove south on Glendale Boulevard and soon found himself driving through the gates of Forest Lawn Memorial Park.

A security guard gave him the once-over as he climbed out of the Packard in the empty parking lot.

"No picture-taking," the guard cautioned Trace.

"Do I look like a goddamn tourist?" he grumbled.

Trace lit a slim cigar after the guard passed and, hands thrust deep in his trouser pockets, began strolling through the cemetery like any other man would stroll through a playground.

"Among the dead," he said to himself and smiled. It was the title of one of his favorite novels.

He came upon a locked area that was not accessible to the public. There were grave markers inside the secure compound and when his weary eyes rested upon one particular pale green marker he knew he had his poem. He pulled a wire-bound memo notebook from his coat pocket and leaned against a headstone as he wrote the five simple lines:

Bogart Sleeps Here

Born on Christmas Day in 1899
Died on January 14, two years before I was born
His middle name was DeForest
The vase next to his headstone holds no flowers

"It's terrific! I knew you could do it!" Marcel gushed on the phone.

"It's shit," Trace complained.

"No, it's very good."

"Whatever."

Trace hung up, poured a slug of Potter's Vodka into a shot glass, and wondered why he pursued words for a living.

Poor Sonofabitch

"You know that I have to write about this," Trace called out to Lisa from the bathroom. He finished brushing his teeth and, glancing to the mirror as he replaced the toothbrush, he saw a face he couldn't recognize. It was his own face but a much younger version.

When Trace returned to the bedroom, Lisa was half-asleep. Her long, slender legs were entwined in the soft brown bed sheets like orphaned tree limbs littering the desert floor.

"You know I have to write about this," he repeated. "I always wanted to write about someone having an affair but, having never experienced one until now, I never trusted myself to be honest with those kinds of emotions on paper."

She opened her eyes and smiled at him. "Is that what this is? We're having an affair?"

Trace hiked his shoulders and squinted at the wallpaper as if he thought he might find an answer in the wavy, cream-colored horizontal lines.

"I don't know what 'this' is. It's something, isn't it?"

"Yes, it is. What are you going to write then? About us? About 'this'?"

"Maybe just a short story," he said, lighting a cigarette and admiring her legs.

Trace took a hard pull on the cigarette and exhaled a plume of smoke that descended upon Lisa like a thick, white cloud. Trace apologized profusely and moved to the balcony door, sliding it open to allow a stiff breeze to enter the hotel room that had been his home for the last four years. It had been raining for five punishing days. Los Angeles had never seen such a steady deluge, or so the TV weathermen kept saying.

Trace stood on the balcony in his white cotton bathrobe and watched as another storm system moved in from the west, engulfing the glass and steel high rises of the L.A. skyline, causing them to vanish from the horizon right before his eyes.

"The skyline just disappeared," he said, poking his head back into the room through the opening in the balcony door. "More heavy rain headed this way."

Lisa didn't reply. She was either sleeping, Trace thought, or trying to process this strange and exhilarating thing that had happened to them over the last five days. He wondered how his wife Josephine was going to take the news he had to deliver and how he was going to present the grim information.

"I don't think she can possibly be surprised," Trace told Lisa earlier in the day as they lay entangled in each other's bodies. "The marriage has been dead for the last two years and she knows it as well as I do."

"When we met," Lisa sighed sweetly, "you gave me no indication of your availability. I mean, I knew you were married but you seemed genuinely interested in getting to know me so I didn't know whether we were just going to have a few fun days in bed or something more serious. You hinted at something more serious on Friday night."

The rain had only just begun that Friday evening when Lisa arrived at Trace's hotel room. Now, five days later, the drumming rain had caused sodden hillsides to give way, carrying a swimming pool in Bel-Air into a ravine. Floodwaters from the Santa Clara

River had carved away a hundred and fifty feet of runway at Santa Paula Airport. There had been waterspouts over the Santa Monica Bay and the National Weather Service had posted tornado warnings for the entire Los Angeles basin for two days.

Trace tossed the spent cigarette into a rain puddle on the balcony and returned to the room. Lisa stirred beneath the sheets. He was glad she was not asleep.

"Does the magazine you work for want you to write about Hunter Thompson?" she asked.

"Everyone and their mother is writing about his death already," Trace said. "I don't know what I have to contribute. I can say that a great deal of what I know about writing I learned from reading Thompson but everyone else is saying the same thing. This is as big as Fitzgerald's passing."

He poured a shot glass to the rim with Potter's Vodka from a $3.99 pint bottle he picked up at the corner liquor store. The bar at the Glendale Day's Inn didn't open until six in the evening and there was no store of any kind on the hotel premises. He ruined his least favorite pair of shoes going out in the torrential downpour to pick up cigarettes and the vodka but he didn't care. He had Lisa in his bed and with her presence came a restoration of who he was and where he was going in life.

"Poor sonofabitch," he exhaled as he slid between the sheets and wrapped himself up in Lisa.

"Why do you say that?"

"It was what Dorothy Parker said when she went to the mortuary in Culver City to view Fitzgerald's body. 'Poor sonofabitch.' That's all I can say about Hunter Thompson."

He rolled over on his side and she studied his face in the half-glow of the soft candlelight that filled the room.

"Poor sonofabitch," she repeated.

On Dangerous Ground

Before emerging from his car in the church parking lot, Trace slid a fresh clip into the 9mm and eased it into the canvas bag along with his notebooks, tape recorders – he always carried two in case the batteries abruptly died on one of them – and a pack of smokes.

The Vineland Boyz street gang controlled the North Hollywood neighborhood where the small Catholic church was located. Even though their numbers had been diminished by a series of recent police raids, Trace knew there were always wanna-be gangbangers roaming the streets looking to impress the chieftains through mindless acts of turf-protecting violence. The gun, within easy reach in the canvas bag slung over his shoulder, made Trace feel more confident while treading through hostile, alien ground.

Since the church parking lot hosted the media circus – news vans, always freshly scrubbed, with their microwave antennas jutting into the gray morning sky – Trace was forced to park on a narrow side street. The homes on the street were two- and three-bedroom cracker boxes, Lockheed-era housing, single-family dwellings hastily assembled during the Second World War to accommodate the influx of defense plant workers from out of state.

World War Two, Trace thought as he climbed out of the car. Now there was a time when war was good for the economy.

Sixty years after the cessation of hostilities in Europe and the South Pacific, the defense plants of Burbank and El Segundo had dried up and blown away. The middle-class neighborhoods that had grown up around the war factories were still occupied by the middle class but mostly young first-time home buyers who didn't mind the fact that every third or fourth home on their block housed a Mexican-American family with ties to the street gang culture. The houses proudly owned by the white suburbanites were easy to spot. They were the ones with the signs posted on the front lawn announcing the top-notch alarm system protecting the house.

The modern day equivalent of a moat, Trace thought as he strolled toward the Catholic church.

Trace won the freelance assignment for *City View* magazine by putting a unique spin on the headline-grabbing story of the weeping Virgin Mary statue.

"I'm a lapsed Catholic," Trace confessed to the editor.

The editor liked the point-of-view for a first-person narrative. It was a lie. But for a buck a word and the guarantee of a two-thousand-word feature there was no end to the lies Trace was willing to assume.

The tears flowing from the crowd assembled around the statue in the church courtyard were so copious that Trace could have floated through the front doors upon their waves.

A reporter for the local NBC affiliate – Trace recognized her as the former child star of a family sitcom from the Eighties – waved a microphone in the face of a plump Hispanic woman.

"It's a miracle," the woman blubbered. "It's an affirmation of faith, is what it is."

Trace leaned into a newspaper photographer he was acquainted with and spoke out of the side of his mouth.

"Her tears are real," he said. "That statue I'm not so sure about. Do you know if they allow smoking on the church grounds?"

The photographer rolled his eyes and evaporated into the crowd.

"Fuck you, too," Trace muttered. "Fuck you very much."

Trace reached into the canvas bag with one hand and groped for his pack of cigarettes. It was at that precise moment that someone in the crowd shouted.

"Look! The tears of the Holy Mother are turning to blood!"

The small crowd — twenty-five people at best, Trace measured, excluding the media whores — surged forward as one, a collective mass conspiring to bring him to his knees on the cold concrete surface of the church courtyard. Trace struggled to remain upright but the bag slipped from his shoulder. The reverential murmurings of the devoutly faithful were suddenly drowned out by the accidental discharge of Trace's gun as the canvas bag hit the concrete.

Most people ducked for cover. Some actually ran, fleeing wildly into the parking lot of the Ralph's grocery store adjoining the church. And many simply glared at Trace in shocked disbelief.

"It was an accident," Trace said to no in particular. "And I have a permit for it."

"You brought a gun onto church grounds?" a voice from the crowd assailed him.

"I'm sure it's not the first time," Trace mumbled as he stooped over to collect his belongings. There was a neat hole in the canvas bag where the slug passed through. His eyes followed the trajectory of the bullet and came to rest on a pane of stained glass above the church doors.

The NBC reporter stepped forward.

"Don't I know you?" she said with a flirtatious flip of her blonde mane.

"Maybe," Trace grumbled, fishing in his wallet. He extracted a twenty-dollar bill and pressed it into her palm. "Do me a favor and put this in the church collection box before you go, will ya?"

Her eyes suspiciously followed his.

"You shot the church window?" she hissed in a half-whisper.

"Oh, for Christ's sake, it wasn't intentional."

He walked back to his car at a brisk clip, berating himself along the way for not asking the former child star out for a drink.

Bowling Trophy

"Where's my damn award?" Trace growled into the phone.

"Come down and get it," Evan said in an agreeable voice. "We'll have lunch."

"I can't come down there. You know I'm stuck in Vacaville."

Trace was pacing the living room of the small apartment with manic fury, gripping the telephone handset so aggressively that it wouldn't have surprised him in the least if the damn thing exploded in his hand.

"Doesn't Vacaville mean Cow Town in Spanish?" Evan laughed.

Go ahead and laugh, chucklehead, Trace thought. I'll walk from Vacaville to L.A. just so I can shove that hunk of junk trophy up your narrow ass.

"How's that working out for you?" Evan asked. He was skirting the issue again.

The year was 2000. Two months prior Trace won his first prize for writing, an Erotic Writers Award for a dark short story about a lesbian stalker called *Shadows*. Trace refused to attend the awards show in Manhattan. He barely had enough cash on hand for a pack of cigarettes in those days, let alone airfare to New York.

Evan Banks, Trace's editor at *Soft Sheets Erotica* magazine, attended the show and picked up the award on Trace's behalf. Two months later the award was still resting on Evan's desk in L.A. instead of in its rightful place on Trace's desk.

"How's what working out for me?" Trace snapped.

"Cow Town. Vacaville."

Vacaville had proven to be a cursed town for Trace and his second wife, Josephine. Nothing but miserable bad luck followed them from the day they moved to the cloistered community fifty miles north of San Francisco. It had been billed as a temporary move "for a change of scenery" but on Josephine's second day at her new secretarial job in the Solano County Courthouse she slipped on a spilled soda in the cafeteria and tore the tendon in her left leg and the meniscus in her right knee. Surgery and rehab followed and Trace spent so much time taking care of his bed-ridden wife that if it weren't for her state disability checks they would have no income at all.

"Jo took the accident as some kind of sign from the universe that she wasn't meant to be a nine-to-fiver," Trace explained to Evan with a deep sigh. "We've been humping along like a couple of wounded dogs just trying to meet the bills with what I get from my magazine assignments – which are getting fewer and fewer these days – and the stuff she sells on eBay."

"Oh? What does she sell?"

"Lampwork glass beads. She makes them. She has a torch and a workshop at her mom and dad's house here in town. But she's only just now getting her name established in the bead world so her stuff's not selling for big bucks yet. She used to do oil paintings, too, but that's on hold for now."

Trace paused to light a cigar and then launched the conversation back on track.

"When are you sending me my award, Evan?"

"I need to have a duplicate made first."

"For what?" Trace barked.

"For me. I was your editor on that piece so the award is as much mine as yours."

"You have got be fucking kidding me, Evan. Your name's not on the award."

"Two weeks. Give me two weeks to get it back from the duplicator and then I'll UPS it to you."

Evan was true to his word. Two weeks later UPS delivered a large box to Trace's door. Inside, wrapped in sheets of newsprint, was Trace's Erotic Writers Award. He propped it on the desk next to the framed photo of Jack London.

"Look at that," Trace said to Jo when she returned home from a long day at the torch. He shook his head ruefully. "It looks like a goddamn bowling trophy."

"Indeed it does," Jo agreed. "What's for dinner?"

Stalag Dracula

Trace could smell the desperation on the two men when he walked into the restaurant. A vaporous cloud of wretched hopelessness hung over their table, the detritus of their failed careers taking the form of a black storm front that threatened to explode with violent fury at any moment.

If I can see it, Trace thought, surely their investors can see it, as well as their wives, friends, and their associates in the low-budget film community. Their children can see it. Their bill collectors can sense it. Even their pets probably shied away from them for fear of that loathsome smell wafting from their human frames.

Trace knew that Jack Smalls, sitting to the left of Gray Hubler in the booth at Marie Callender's, had been living off credit cards and bank loans for two years now. He knew next to nothing about Gray Hubler except for the basic facts: He was a camera operator for *Gunsmoke* in the Sixties and then he gravitated toward the low-budget indie market, slaving as director of photography on over two hundred instantly forgettable pieces of schlock with laughable titles like *Mistress Dracula's Blood Orgy*.

"That was back in the days when we had drive-ins to take our product," Gray explained to Trace when they first met a week prior. "Today all of the low-budget stuff is direct to video. I was in Blockbuster the other day and saw five of my movies on the shelves, still renting after all this time."

Somehow Smalls and Hubler had parasitically attached themselves to "a group of Beverly Hills investors" who wanted to invest in a package of three-hundred-thousand-dollar horror films.

"It's real money," Jack told Trace.

Trace was three weeks behind on his rent at the hotel. Smalls and Hubler were offering him five hundred against seventy-five hundred dollars for a horror screenplay that they could take to their investors for a green light. First, however, Trace had to write a treatment – a concise synopsis of the story and all of its dramatic beats – before they could approve the concept and send him away with a check for five hundred in his briefcase and a momentary reprieve from the wolves howling at the door.

Hubler was leaning heavily toward a concept of his own.

"A vampire story set in a concentration camp," Hubler suggested to Trace. "That way we get two horror elements in one: the vampire and the horror of the concentration camp."

Smalls nodded his head in eager agreement. He always deferred to Hubler.

"So, you're thinking *Stalag 17* meets *Dracula*?" Trace offered.

"Exactly! But with less of the humor of *Stalag 17*." Hubler beamed and turned to Smalls. "You're right. This guy's good."

Trace wanted to crawl under the table but as long as that five hundred dollar lure was in front of him he was going to stay put. A writer for hire never walks away from a job prospect until the money fails to materialize.

Jack Smalls took a long swallow of his iced tea and leaned forward excitedly.

"This is really great because the victims of the vampire can be the camp guards. The audience will be all – 'Yeah, yeah, yeah' – to see them get killed."

There were practical reasons that Hubler and Smalls were sold on *Stalag Dracula*. Hubler had access to an affordable location, an abandoned camp for wayward youth on the outskirts of the Mojave Desert. Further, Hubler's biggest box office smashes had been sex and blood soaked vampire tales.

This means that Hubler is riding his own coattails, Trace calculated, banking on his past successes to compel those Beverly Hills investors to scribble out a check for three hundred grand. It didn't feel right. It never did with guys like this. It suddenly struck Trace as funny that the hustle and con of the low-budget horror market seemed to be a man's game. One rarely met women down this dark alley in the slums of the film industry. Women seem to have more sense than to dick around with a waste of film that was only going to net them a few grand in the long run. Give a woman a shot at producing a motion picture and she wants to make the next *Terms of Endearment*, not *Stalag Dracula*.

Trace sat on the edge of his bed that evening and cleaned his gun while watching an old VHS of *Stalag 17* for inspiration. William Holden in his prime, before the ravages of drink transformed his face into a Dorian Gray-like visage of cruel mockery. The critics and film historians said the former matinee idol had developed "character" in his rugged face as he grew older but what he really developed was a fondness for alcoholic binges that was written in the crags and crevasses and wrinkles and the deep-set hollow of his eyes.

Trace spent the next two days writing the movie treatment, enticed by the promise of that check for five hundred, invigorated by the prospect of paying his rent and having one less financial monster looming behind the door.

The story was pure simplicity: Gestapo High Command is frightened by a series of brutal murders at one of their POW camps for captured American officers. Someone or something is viciously and systematically murdering the camp guards, draining their corpulent Germanic bodies of blood. The buzz going around the camp is that a vampire is responsible for the heinous slaughter so an undercover agent is sent in to investigate.

"Not just any undercover man," Trace explained to Hubler and Smalls when they met after the treatment was complete. "This guy is a descendant of the great vampire slayer Van Helsing. He knows his blood-sucking fiends."

As soon as those words slipped from Trace's lips, the deal was dead.

"Universal released that Van Helsing movie last summer and it absolutely bombed," Hubler said.

Jack Smalls nodded his assent and sipped his iced tea.

"So, we change it from Van Helsing to just any old vampire killer," Trace offered, feeling the five hundred floating away into the ether – or into that black cloud over the heads of Smalls and Hubler.

Hubler shook his head vigorously. "No. You set it up too well. It really, really works. This movie can't be done without Van Helsing and no one will touch anything with those two words in it right now."

"It's my treatment," Trace argued. "I can rewrite it to be anything I want. Look, guys, we're just in the embryonic stage of development here."

Smalls and Hubler exchanged a glance across the table. Trace felt betrayed. He had known Smalls for twenty-seven years and expected some kind of tip-off if this was going to be yet another low-budget filmmaking jerk-off session.

"Do you have any other ideas?" Hubler asked. "Maybe a werewolf story? I was involved in *The Howling*, you know."

"And what if we change it from a concentration camp to just a regular prison?" Smalls chimed in. "A concentration camp is too bleak and dark."

Trace leaned back in his chair, took a long and thoughtful pause as he sipped his coffee, and wished that he were anywhere else but here.

"Try this on for size," he pitched. "A super hero concept. A prison on the outskirts of the desert but not just any prison. This is a high security prison that holds all of the world's most dangerous super villains – "

Hubler leaned forward in his chair. "I'm liking this."

Smalls nodded his head.

" – and someone is killing the super villains, someone or something within the prison walls," Trace continued. "And so a retired super hero, a man who has done battle at one time or another with all of these super villains, is sent in to find out who is killing the bad guys. After all, society needs its villains in order to function, to maintain social order."

There was radiant light in Gray Hubler's eyes. The cloud was lifting.

"This is good. We may not have to go the direct to video route on this one. We might be able to get matching funding from the Sci-Fi Channel on this and do it for a million instead of three hundred thousand."

When Trace returned home one hour later — after much animated banter with Hubler and Smalls about the "powers" of the super villains — there was a Three Day Notice To Pay Rent Or Quit affixed to the door of his Extended Stays hotel room.

There was no way Trace could muster the creativity and the energy to write yet another speculative treatment for free in three days; in fact, Jack had said at the end of the meeting that they wouldn't be able to meet Trace until later next week.

He thought about taking a cab into Hollywood and getting hammered at The Drunkard Duck, a favorite hangout of writers for decades. It was rumored that Nathanael West and Scott Fitzgerald bent their elbows at the plush bar when they, too, were trying to catch a ride on the Hollywood merry-go-round. But he didn't need the inspiration of the ghosts of West and Fitzgerald to write the treatment because he had already decided that he wasn't going to do it. There would be no immediate gain from writing it.

"Congratulations," he muttered as he poured a dose of Black Velvet into a shot glass emblazoned with the words HOORAY FOR HOLLYWOOD. "You just wasted two days of your life."

This was the predicament he always found himself in: How does one balance possible career advancement against immediate needs? And how much career advancement can be wrestled from penning the screenplay for a low-budget horror film, even one with super heroes and super villains in it?

This was a game better and more enthusiastically played by people much younger than Trace. He was forty-seven years old, divorced, with a twelve-year-old daughter he rarely saw or spoke to. He had worked as a professional writer for over a decade but now the jobs were getting fewer and further between and he had no other bankable or reliable skills except as a producer of feature documentaries for television and theatrical release. The documentary gigs, though, took a year or more to complete and only paid on the back end. He published a novel, *Northfield Through A Haze*, an opium-laced recounting of the final days of the James-Younger Gang, but the quarterly royalties weren't enough to put even a dent in his staggering deficit.

And then there were the Dan Knight Stories. Dan Knight was Trace's alter ego, a fictional creation who appeared in a series of short stories that Trace wrote in his leisure time for his website. The details of his life, both personal and professional, were spilled out in the Dan Knight stories with all the careless abandon of stray auto parts on the freeway after a great pile-up, the kind of mangled wreckage that sends L.A. commuters into a full-bore SIG alert and gives the morning news anchors something to be concerned about other than the latest celebrity gossip and the little abandoned puppy that's going to be put down by the Humane Society if you don't make a call to Adopt-A-Pet right fucking now.

Trace began writing the stories as a tool to mitigate the creative silences between magazine and documentary assignments. In the freelance world such work is called "writing on spec" – writing on the speculation that one just might have a final product worth selling.

He downed the shot of smooth Canadian whiskey, poured another, and moved to the south-facing balcony of his fifth-floor

floor hotel room. Night had long fallen and the lights of Dodger Stadium in Chavez Ravine hummed in the distance. The Dodgers were in a home stand against the San Francisco Giants that evening.

There was a thundering boom like incoming artillery or mortar fire and then the night sky over Chavez Ravine lit up in a dazzling array of color. Another boom followed and the fireworks display commenced in full.

The Dodgers must have won, Trace thought.

He carried the shot glass and bottle of Black Velvet to the balcony and leaned against the iron railing. The sky continued to crackle and pop and burst with color for a full thirty minutes while Trace observed with dispassionate interest.

When the fireworks finally subsided a noxious smell lingered in the air above the city, a scent not unlike the odor of crackling desperation.

Trace Goes to Urgent Care

"It's not diaper rash, Doctor."

"Yes, I can see that. She has another red patch here. When did that first appear?"

"I noticed that this morning when I was bathing her. The rash gets real red – I mean, bright, bright red – when she gets in the bath."

Trace listened to the conversation through the exam room curtain with a growing sense of irritation. The doctor had been examining the six-month-old baby for fifteen minutes and still didn't have the diagnosis down. Trace knew to expect a long wait at Urgent Care on a Sunday afternoon but two-and-a-half hours had now passed and the pain wasn't letting up.

Ninety minutes earlier he was encamped in the waiting room – after paying one hundred dollars for the pleasure of the visit – with a lot of parents and their cranky newborns and one old man reading the Sunday *L.A. Times* with such a casual air you would think he was in his living room.

A thin, matronly woman wearing a black Gucci jogging suit entered through the main door and headed for the check-in counter hurriedly. On her heels was a young Salvadoran woman in a simple pastel-colored T-shirt and white cotton sweats. She was keeping her left arm elevated. A strand of packaging tape had been applied to a gash on her wrist. It looked to Trace as if she had accidentally put her arm through a window, probably while cleaning it.

"No, she doesn't have a driver's license," Trace heard the Gucci woman telling the desk nurse. "She doesn't have any form of identification at all and she doesn't speak English. I'm paying for this."

Yeah, I'll bet you are, Trace thought. I'm sure the girl can't afford the one hundred dollar fee on the five bucks an hour you pay her to clean your house.

The parents and their babies were seen first and dismissed quickly. Trace knew the type because he was one of them once; anxious fathers and mothers who detect pneumonia in every sniffle from baby, bronchitis in every cough.

But by the time Trace was finally admitted to an exam room the doctor seemed perplexed by the rash on the infant he was treating in the adjacent partition, a perplexity that was delaying Trace's treatment by another twenty minutes.

"Look here," the doctor spoke through the curtain. "There's some blistering in the rash here. Hm."

"Oh, for Christ's sake," Trace muttered.

"Hello?" he called through the curtain.

No answer.

"Hello?" He beckoned once more. "Doctor?"

The doctor answered after a lingering beat. "Yes?"

"It's psoriasis! The baby has psoriasis."

Another pregnant pause. "Well. Hm. Yes, I think it is psoriasis."

Ten minutes later Trace was walking out the door with drops for his infected ear, steroid nasal spray for his sinus condition, and an extra cache of Triamcinolone ointment for his severe psoriasis.

Smoke

The Santa Monica Pier was cluttered with the usual batch of late summer tourists, plump and pasty-skinned Midwestern families ambling about in their Universal Studios T-shirts with mini-camcorders strapped to their wrists. Trace hated tourists and always felt like one himself whenever he visited such L.A. landmarks, which inspired a jaded "I would rather be anywhere but here" persona just in case somebody actually did mistake him for a tourist.

Josephine suggested they walk along the shore, maybe sit for a while and just enjoy the waves rolling in. There was a red tide in the Santa Monica Bay that afternoon and earlier they had enjoyed the sight of a school of dolphins feeding close to shore; so close, in fact, that the L.A. County Lifeguards rolled out their boat – which resembled a fishing trawler, oddly enough – to make sure the dolphins didn't swim too close to the slim handful of human waders in the noxious, chemical-filled bay.

The City of Santa Monica long ago banned smoking on the beach so when Trace settled down in the lush sand on the towel Josephine brought along for just that purpose, he immediately began searching for things to do with his hands. He poked at the sand with his walking stick and unearthed seashells. He sifted the sand out of a batch of half-shells and gingerly placed them on the hotel towel.

This is a good project, he thought. He needed a project, something to do with his time while he lazed at the beach because just lazing at the beach in and of itself wasn't very challenging or interesting to Trace. It was August 2004. He had writing assignments to think about but the deadlines were so far off in the future that he could afford the luxury of not fretting over them. Not now, not during the day at the beach he had promised to both himself and Jo. He dug the tip of his walking stick into the sand and pushed himself to his feet.

He didn't know that Josephine was snapping pictures of him as he shuffled along the shoreline, cell phone holster on his hip, stick in hand to steady his arthritic gait, collecting sea shells where he could find them obscured in the sand and washing the residue off of them in the breaking tidewaters.

"Too many mussel shells," he complained to Jo when he dropped off the fifth batch of shells.

"There are crabs in this one," Josephine said as she examined a large shell Trace discovered a few yards away.

Trace peered at it from a safe distance — he didn't like small, crawling things — and, sure enough, at least three microscopic crabs were frantically scrambling around the interior of the shell.

"I'll be damned," Trace said. And he walked away to continue his hunt for shells.

When he finally got bored, he stuffed the cleaned shells into his shoulder bag and suggested that they should begin the drive back to Glendale soon before the evening commute began.

Strolling through the Third Street Promenade — an open-air shopping pavilion anchored mostly by trendy apparel shops and restaurants that Trace wouldn't be caught dead in — he paused to light a cigarette.

"Are you sure they allow smoking here?" Jo asked. She didn't smoke and she frequently let Trace know how his habit unnerved her.

"They only banned smoking on the beach," Trace said.

But when it came time to extinguish the cigarette he could find no public ashtrays like they have on busy Brand Boulevard in Glendale. The sidewalks of the Third Street Promenade appeared to be devoid of spent cigarette butts. He didn't know what to do, how to discreetly snub out his smoke. It was as if he had landed on The Planet of Non-Smokers.

Coming toward him was a plump, middle-aged woman in a wheelchair being pushed by another matronly woman. Trace needed to get out of their path and to get rid of the damn cigarette. He spied a crushed butt on the sidewalk just outside the display window of one of those chic boutiques. He pretended to be eyeing the display window while covertly crunching out the cigarette with the heel of his shoe.

"Why did you do that?" Jo asked when he caught up with her on the walkway.

"They don't have any goddamn ashtrays around here," he grumbled. "I had no choice."

"Well, you should have seen the look that woman gave you," she said.

"Oh, fuck her," Trace said with a scowl. "She probably got herself into a wheelchair by giving someone a dirty look like that."

Josephine sighed and they continued on for a few moments until Trace broke the silence by bringing up a more pleasant topic, perhaps a side trip on the way home to a favorite old watering hole of theirs. His treat. It was the only way he knew how to admit that he could be an asshole sometimes.

Henry Miller in the Rain

The rain came down upon the old man's smooth and hairless head like stinging needles of punishment. When he saw the yellow glow of the Western Union sign in the night sky he momentarily forgot about the storm and the wet clothing that clung to his wizened skin like death's wraith and became lost in thoughts about Henry Miller.

"Stop me if you've heard this before," the old man told Trace over the phone when he returned home. "Henry Miller worked at Western Union in New York for four years. He wrote his first book during a three-week vacation from Western Union."

"He left Western Union in 1924," Trace responded like a student called upon to complete the master's thought, "determined never to take a job again, and devoted his entire energy to writing."

The old man was still in his damp clothing. Juanita had a fire roaring in the rugged stone fireplace. He carried the phone closer to the warmth of the flames.

"You remind me of Henry Miller, Trace," he said. "Accompanied by great poverty, you still manage to write wonderful prose."

"And sometimes I get paid for the effort," Trace said with a self-deprecating sigh.

"At least you're not selling your book door to door like Miller had to do with *Mezzotints*."

"Considering how slumped my sales have been, Max, that might not be a bad option."

It was 9:30 in the evening in Florida, where Max Wiesner was calling from. In L.A., it was 6:30 and the sun was beginning its descent into the Pacific. Trace stood on the balcony of his hotel room, cell phone painfully pressed to his ear, and watched the sky succumb to a reddish-pink sunset.

Trace awoke that morning with what he diagnosed as another cloying hangover but the dull roar in his head, just behind his left ear, said otherwise. He had eighty-five dollars in the bank, magazines were rejecting his pitches like batters refusing to swing, and a much-needed visit to the doctor's office was sure to tap him out.

The dull roar gave way by mid-afternoon to a stabbing pain deep in his ear and momentary losses of equilibrium. There could be no doubt about it. He had to go to the doctor.

Trace was diagnosed with a severe middle ear infection, caused and compounded by a sinus infection. He was prescribed Zyrtec-D for the sinus problem and was placed on a full course of antibiotic therapy. He wrote a check for the office visit and the medications, setting him back a hundred and fifty, determined to worry about how to cover the check when he was feeling better. The doctor told him it would be three or four days before that most welcome event would occur.

"I'm getting vibed by you all the way out here in Tampa Bay," Max said when he phoned Trace that evening. "Is everything okay?"

Max Wiesner was long retired from his career as a classics professor, an occupation he came to after stints as an infantryman in the Korean War, a rodeo clown on the Southwest circuit, and some dubious work as a "tour boat" operator in the Florida Keys.

When Doubleday was preparing to publish Trace's first novel *Northfield Through A Haze*, Max, whom Trace had never met nor even heard of, offered a favorable blurb for the dust jacket after a former student passed a galley proof of the book onto him.

"It's a fine book, an outstanding first achievement," Max wrote Trace. "I would be pleased to prepare a fitting response to your accomplishment as it has been years since I have seen my own name in print. I'm getting on in years and I would like to be remembered as a man who had at least some small impact on American literature."

Over the last two years Max and Trace had enjoyed weekly telephone calls. Max was fascinated by Trace's daily struggles as a writer for hire and Trace enjoyed hearing the colorful tales of Max Wiesner's life before academia beckoned him.

"I have a goddamn middle ear infection and I just spent every dollar I had left in the bank on a doctor's visit and medications," Trace told Max. "Maybe that's why you're getting vibed by me."

Max was accustomed to hearing Trace's tales of economic peril and had never offered to intercede. For some reason, though, this episode had an impact on the old man.

"Give me the name of the nearest Western Union and I'll wire you some bread," Max offered.

Trace wanted to protest but he had no idea where his next paycheck was coming from. He expected that Max would wire the cash in the morning but two hours later the phone rang and, after the banter about Henry Miller, Max detailed his adventure.

"We're having a major thunderstorm here tonight, got soaked walking from the car to the door of the store where they have a Western Union office. I got to the Western Union office five minutes before closing, only to have the door slammed and locked in my face."

"Ah, Jesus, Max, I didn't expect you to go out in that kind of weather to wire me money."

"Don't worry about it, Trace. I'll send it first thing in the morning. Fifty bucks. It's all I can spare until the eagle shits on the first of the month. I hope it helps. As Granny said while pissing in the ocean, 'Ever little bit helps when you're trying to drown yer no account husband'."

Trace laughed and settled down on the bed, popping another tab of Zyrtec to stop the kettledrum in his head. He washed it down with a shot of Potter's Vodka.

"A lot of good ideas were generated by getting out of the house and sucking up some fresh, moist air," Max continued. "I'm thinking of writing some short stories about the days when Juanita and I first courted."

Max had been married to Juanita for thirty-five years. They had two grown daughters to be proud of. Teresa was a commercial airline pilot and Estelle followed in her father's footsteps as a classics professor. Max and Juanita were spending the waning days of their retirement shuffling from one doctor's appointment to the next.

"Juanita had both a mammogram and one of those echo things today," he said. "She has something very large, ugly, and sore in there. Her radiologist went ballistic when he saw it, so she's going into the hospital for a biopsy ASAP."

"Oh, Jesus, Max. I'm sorry."

"I'm rattled, Trace. That mass is as large as my ashtray and it'll hold eight cigarettes at once. And then on Friday the goddamn doctors have me galloping on a treadmill while wired for sound and graphics. The ticker ain't getting any better. We have good neighbors to feed our cats and dogs should we become inpatients simultaneously but it's been our habit to take turns getting sick."

Trace felt horrible now. It wasn't the ear infection that caused him pain. It was Max's tale of advancing age, stories that must come to a close, lives that inevitably end. He wasn't confronting his own mortality – he did that several times a day every day of his life – but rather the mortality of a friend and of his friend's wife.

"Seeing that Western Union sign tonight brought Henry Miller up from the depths," Max said wistfully. "I could see him taking Anais Nin by her lovely little hand as they danced on the cobblestones."

Trace grappled for a pack of cigarettes on the nightstand. He felt affection for the old man and affection for living things did not come easily or painlessly for Trace.

"Check your Western Union first thing in the morning," Max said after a considered pause. "There'll be fifty bucks there. Get yourself a decent breakfast."

"Don't Take Your Guns To Town"
A Dan Knight Story

"It's time for you to die," Dan Knight snarled at the corpulent editor. "I hope you understand that it's nothing personal."

Dan grabbed the edge of the desk with both hands and pounced to his feet. Raw menace was dripping from him like molasses on a thick stack of flapjacks. His hand darted inside his slate gray Clipper Mist overcoat and when it reappeared he was gripping the System Automatic 9mm revolver. His hand had never been more calm and steady as the moment when he leveled the gun barrel at Oscar's plump and ruddy face. It would be a clean kill. One shot.

From behind the desk where he ran herd on a batch of mongrel freelance journalists, the overfed editor of the "automotive lifestyles" magazine made a barking sound like a seal. Dan's finger twitched inside the trigger housing of the revolver and… and… and….

BACKSPACE BACKSPACE BACKSPACE BACKSPACE

Dan's finger twitched inside the trigger housing of the revolver. He could see the dread realization in Oscar's eyes, the fatal resignation that… that… that…

Trace stopped typing and stared blankly at the computer monitor. The Dan Knight stories were beginning to make him feel fragmented.

After writing ten Dan Knight stories for his website, Trace found a temporary market for the pieces with Slumming Angel Press, a San Francisco imprint that published a quarterly anthology of modern and reissued pulp fiction shorts. Slumming Angel only paid ten cents a word and three comp copies of the magazine but a dollar is a dollar and a clip is another notch in the headboard.

Trace lit a Marlboro and boiled water in the microwave for instant coffee. One hundred words away from completing the new Dan Knight tale and he was stuck. It wasn't writers block. Trace didn't believe in that bullshit. The Dan Knight stories were easy enough to write because they were pure autobiography with one notable exception: Dan Knight always resolved conflict with gunplay. Like Trace, Dan was a writer for hire in the vast disconnected wasteland of Southern California, a man who sometimes sold his skills as an investigative journalist to bidders outside the magazine racket when the realities of economic law required it.

Trace flinched when the microwave issued four sharp electronic beeps. He was still tender from the middle ear infection he endured a week before but that was child's play compared to what his old friend Max Wiesner was going through back in Tampa Bay. Max's wife, Juanita, had a biopsy performed and the report had just come back. It was definitely carcinoma and because the lump in her breast had grown so rapidly and so large, a radical mastectomy was the only option.

When Trace received the news about Juanita from Max, the angry edge he had been wearing all day began to dissipate into a puddle at his feet. He needed that edge to finish the Dan Knight story.

Trace poured a heaping spoonful of instant Folgers into the coffee mug, dumped in two teaspoons of sugar and Coffee Mate, and returned to the desk and the beckoning keyboard.

His eyes fell upon the latest letter from Gloria, the demented stalker he acquired after the publication of *Northfield Through A Haze*. He decided to read the letter once more. He opened it gingerly, knowing and fearing that it might turn out to be evidence someday.

"Do you realize the obsession?" Gloria wrote to Trace. "I'm so wanting to know what the point is and if there is a risk why isn't it confronted? Why is this risk a threat? Is it because we are powerless or powerful?"

The letter arrived inside a bulky package that contained a book of graphic sexual art titled *Erotica Universalis*.

"I'm sending you a little book," Gloria continued in her neat cursive handwriting. "I'm sure you've seen it all in your writing for dirty magazines but maybe you could return it in person. It's part of a set."

Trace lit another cigarette and sipped his coffee.

"Have you ever been to Kentucky?" Gloria asked on the third page of the five-page letter. "Do you want to meet me in Chicago and drive to the fireworks over the Ohio River on 4/23? It is awesome! Then on Sunday we could go to the stables. The facilities and bluegrass really is fascinating. Just trying to secure a date with you to check out something way cool."

Asking someone you've never met — the object of a psychosexual obsession — to fly across country for a tour of the Ohio River was one thing but Gloria always took riveting detours into insanity in her letters and e-mails to Trace.

"I'm a little cautious these days," she continued. "I had to change my phone number because my fictional characters are brain damaged and apparently I was/am requiring a stricter vigilance of paranoia. Unfortunately the U.S. Mail is the only way of communication I feel safe."

Trace carefully folded the letter and slid it back into the envelope. It was postmarked, as always, in Marietta, Ohio, and Trace felt comfort in the great distance between him and Gloria. But after receiving the last letter he felt compelled to take evasive action. He called the home phone number that Gloria had provided and heaved a sigh of relief when it rolled over to her voice mail.

"Gloria, this is Trace calling from Los Angeles," he said in a voice crackling with tension. "Look, you don't know me. We've never met. You've only read some of my articles and my book – and it's not a very good book at that. Why don't you find someone new to obsess on, huh? I hear Norman Mailer isn't doing much these days."

Two hours after leaving the message on Gloria's voice mail, Trace received a terse e-mail from her.

"You're right. Sorry I bothered you. Please return my art book."

Trace had laughed at the last line. He retained and filed away every insane letter, e-mail, and package he ever received from Gloria. There was no way in hell she was getting the book back.

Dan Knight wouldn't have put up with Gloria as long and patiently as Trace did. Dan Knight would have casually hopped a plane to Marietta, Ohio, stalked her down like prey, and sent her miserable soul to the bowels of hell with his 9mm. But Trace wasn't Dan Knight, even though he did own a System Automatic 9mm and when his temper flared it was a good idea to keep a safe distance between Trace and his gun. He would never turn the gun on anyone he cared about. Witnessing his mother's battering at the hands of scores of husbands and boyfriends while growing up instilled within Trace a rage at anyone who even hints of physically abusing a loved one – those were the personality types who needed to fear Trace when he was angry and searching for an outlet.

But as he struggled to complete the latest Dan Knight tale, that angry edge was gone, spurred away into the distance like a runaway mustang by the plight of Max Wiesner's wife back in Florida.

"Fuck it," he said aloud. "I'll finish it tomorrow. It's just another goddamn Dan Knight story."

He tossed the instant coffee down the bathroom sink, popped open a sixteen-ounce can of Miller High Life, and offered a toast to the framed photograph of Humphrey Bogart that rested near his computer monitor. It was a publicity still from the German release of the great Bogie film *In A Lonely Place*. The German translation of the title was written in dark script beneath the photo of Bogart in a tuxedo nursing a drink at a bar:

"Ein Einasmer Ort."

In A Lonely Place.

Rain and Poetry

"It's raining."

"Yep."

"Read me a poem."

"What?"

"I want to get all comfy-cozy in bed under the sheets and listen to you read me a poem."

"Um, okay. Let me just get into my robe and then I need to do a last e-mail check and put the cell phone on charge and – "

"Jesus. Forget I said anything. You fucking ruin it every time."

"Ruin what?"

"I asked you to read me a poem."

"And I said I would – "

" – after. After you do this and do that and probably have one last cigarette and another shot of whatever you're drinking. Go do what you've got to do. I'm going to sleep."

"Goddamnit, Josephine. Fine. Don't go to sleep. I'll read you a fucking poem, for shit sake. Which one? From which book?"

"Forget it. I don't want to put you out."

"Do you have any idea what kind of a day I had today? I do not need this shit from you right now. It looks like the studio is going to change their mind about the script so you can just forget that Malibu summer beach house for now, honey. Pipe dream."

"I'm sorry, Trace."

"What?"

"I said, I'm sorry. I didn't know. You haven't said anything until now."

"Because you didn't fucking ask. All you were interested in was some goddamn poem."

Skunks of the Hollywood Hills

"Did I ever tell you about the time I groped a girl in a pharmacy and she turned out to be a he?" Trace asked.

Pamela stared at him over the rim of her wine glass and simply blinked.

"The moral of that tale," Trace continued, grabbing the bottle by the neck and refilling his glass to the rim, "is that one needs to know the terrain before assuming a comfort level, or something to that effect."

Trace and Pamela were standing on the white marble patio of a luxurious faux Mediterranean villa in a lush Hollywood Hills canyon. Pamela was a television actress – not a very good one but she had the dumb luck to be in a hit TV show, preceded by the lead role in a hit slasher film – and the house represented the pinnacle of her success.

"I've never owned a home of my own," she told Trace. "If it doesn't get any better than this I'm perfectly fine with that because this is all more than I asked for."

"Uh, huh," Trace grunted. He was momentarily preoccupied by thoughts of how he was going to squeeze another two grand out of her. Trace had been working on a screenplay with Pamela for the last year and a half. She was paying him for his efforts and he made sure that there were lots and lots of rewrites and revisions involved because the Packard needed new tires and a paint job. The screenplay was shit, he knew that, a vanity project if there ever was one. But she had the bucks and he had the talent so it was a comfortable relationship as long as no one asked any questions.

"Trace, what does groping a transsexual have to do with my house?"

"Well, I'm just saying, know your terrain. The Hollywood Hills. Lots of wild animals up here."

Pamela laughed. "What kind of animals?"

"First, you have your coyotes. Coyotes are kind of cool in a mystical, Carlos Castaneda sort of way but watch out for the goddamn skunks up here."

Skunks, he informed her as if he knew what he was talking about and should never be questioned, are prone to rabies.

"If you ever see a skunk walking toward you, run."

"Why?" She laughed again.

"Because skunks are anti-social. They don't like humans. The only time a skunk loses its fear of humans and approaches them is when it's mad from rabies. You get bit by a rabid skunk and you'll have to endure a series of painful injections in the stomach with a needle as long as my arm."

"I thought they had a different way of doing that now."

"Not that I heard of."

Trace convinced her to advance him five hundred dollars off the next installment and promised he would return next Tuesday with new pages.

Over the course of the next week, while Trace was pounding away at a screenplay that he knew would get Pamela laughed out of every production office in Hollywood, the actress was developing a morbid dread of skunks.

It started one evening when she returned home late from the studio and saw a large black and white rodent loitering in her driveway. When her headlights sought out the animal, it turned and looked directly into the halogen and then scampered off into a hedgerow. But she could see its beady eyes in the bushes, glaring at her as she stepped out of the Lexus. Pamela bolted to the front door, tripping on the marble steps and breaking a heel in the process.

The next evening, after a long and languid session of autoerotica – Pamela had sworn off men in her life after discovering the joys of batteries and things that go buzz – she sauntered downstairs for a glass of Chardonnay. She turned on the backyard floodlights to proudly survey her new domain and what she saw made her drop her glass on the marble floor.

"There must have been dozens of them," she shrieked in the phone to Trace. "And the smell! My God."

"Sounds like you live near an enclave," Trace mumbled. He was only half listening to her, his nose buried in a Bruce Wagner novel.

"What's an enclave? You always use words I have to go look up."

"A family of skunks, Pamela. Do you know anyone who's selling weed? I'm running kind of low."

Pamela gave him the phone number of a production assistant who had a profitable sideline selling marijuana and male hustlers. Trace assured her that he was only interested in the former.

By Monday Trace had painfully written ten new pages of Pamela's screenplay. It was so bad, so God awful, such a horrible idea but it was her idea and she wanted him to write it and he had bills to pay. When he phoned to confirm their Tuesday meeting she had good news of her own.

"I got rid of the skunks!" she announced.

"Congratulations. What was the trick?"

"I got a dog. It was the weirdest thing, Trace, like fate. I was driving home late one night and when I got up to this one turn in the canyon there was a dog just standing in the middle of the road. I couldn't swerve to avoid hitting him or I'd go off into the canyon so I stopped the car but he just stood there with these soulful eyes staring at me."

"Uh, huh." Trace was taking a hit off a joint he just rolled. The dealer that Pamela turned him onto sold some good shit, so good and intoxicating that he was able to cut back on his liquor tab at the hotel bar.

"I got out of the car," Pamela continued, "and I crouched down low and extended a hand to him. He looked so sad and mangy and you could see his ribs, he hadn't eaten in so long. He's been here for two days now and he's all fat and happy and the skunks have disappeared and – "

"Did this dog have a collar, Pamela?" Trace probed. "What do its ears look like?"

"Kind of pointy."

"A low animal?"

"A what?"

"Is it a small dog?"

"Yes."

"Uh, huh. And where is this dog now?"

"In the backyard."

Trace told her to keep the dog in the backyard until he got to her house. At that time of night he could make the drive from Glendale to the Hollywood Hills in fifteen minutes.

"I hope you haven't named your new dog yet," he mumbled as she answered the front door. "Or bonded with him or any shit like that."

"Why?"

Trace stood at the closed glass door leading to the back yard and glared at the mangy dog resting on the plush lawn. He lit a cigar and looked upon her as if he just discovered that she was of an alien race.

"That, Pamela," he said, "is a goddamn coyote."

Heart Like a Steel Cowboy

Trace felt ensnared in the restaurant booth. Normally he would have had an exit strategy in play by now but this was no normal situation. All he could do was sip his beer and observe in quiet horror as his longtime friend melted down before his eyes.

"Can you believe that my son is thirty-five years old, Trace?" Jack shook his head in amazement. "Thirty-five years old."

Trace had known Jack Smalls for twenty-seven years. They met when Trace was a fledgling screenwriter and Jack was director of development for a production company financed wholly by the Church Of Scientology. Over the years Jack had been a post production supervisor, an assistant director and a producer of indie films, nothing that really shook out to resemble a remarkable or consistent career. Jack was nearing his sixtieth year of his life. He owed a hundred thousand dollars in credit card debt and he was in an almost feral panic.

"So I'm talking to my son the other day and he tells me he just got back from the doctor for his annual exam, right? Now that he's thirty-five he's starting to have some of the same ailments and complaints that I have. Isn't that remarkable?"

"Our bodies do tend to break down as we get older, Jack," Trace said for lack of anything better to say because that's the way it always was with Jack in conversation. Jack ended a statement with a question as a means of drawing you into the conversation, making sure you were paying attention.

"And so we got to talking about how everything in the body is interconnected, how this ache and pain in the back leads to that pain in the knee and the shoulder and – well, I came up with an idea for a play."

"A play, huh?" Trace signaled the waitress for another draft on tap.

"You're a good playwright, Trace. I read *Winter in the Canyon* twice, you know."

Here it comes, thought Trace. The pitch. He was certain it was going to be awful before the concept even sprung from Jack's lips but what could he do? Jack was a friend, a friend for twenty-seven years. You don't abandon someone like that, especially when they're down on their knees.

"So what's the idea for the play?"

Jack pushed aside his soup bowl, took a long gulp of iced tea, and leaned forward as if he were about to reveal something wonderfully prophetic.

"It's a minimalist theatre piece, which is good because low production costs increase the odds of getting the play produced. Imagine a man's life re-enacted through his various body parts."

The waitress delivered Trace's cold stein of beer. He was tempted to chug it back in one swallow but he was never comfortable displaying his proclivity for vast quantities of booze in front of his old friend.

"You have the actors in white jumpsuits emblazoned across the front with the name of the body part they represent."

"Ah, so you would have one actor representing the heart, another the lungs, and so on and so forth and then you put them in conflict with each other," Trace offered. He knew this piece of theatre well. He saw it on *Sesame Street* with his daughter back when he still lived his wife Gina and their kid.

"Exactly!" Jack slapped the table with his beefy palm. "What do you think? Is it something you want to write up? Do you need to think about it?"

Trace sipped his beer, thinking back to the horror movie treatment he'd written for Jack's friend Gray Hubler and still hadn't been paid for. "Let me chew on that one for awhile."

Take your time." Jack waved at an imaginary pest in the air. "You know, Trace, I'm going down the fucking tubes."

"We all are, Jack."

"It's a shame, Trace," Jack said, his eyes getting misty. "You're such a good writer."

"Yeah, well – " Trace took another swallow from his beer and excused himself.

On the way to the men's room Trace passed the restaurant bakery and gave momentary consideration to buying a pie to take back to the hotel but he knew he would only eat a couple slices of it while stoned and let the rest go to waste. He wasn't in a position to throw money around that carelessly, not this week, not this month.

Unzipping himself at the urinal he forced himself to think in the immediate, to just concentrate on relieving his bladder and not give a moment's pause to Jack's awful pitch and what it all meant in the long run. His eyes wandered across the tile wall in front of the urinal. With a felt tip pen someone had scrawled the words HEART LIKE A STEEL COWBOY on the wall. The calligraphy was very neat and precise. Someone had taken their time to display those words on the bathroom wall.

Seafood

"Do you know what you want?"

"That's a profound question."

"I was talking about the menu, Trace."

"Well, Josephine, I'm giving serious consideration to the Chilean sea bass."

"I didn't know you like fish."

"There're a lot of things you don't know about me. Are you finished with the painting yet?"

"No. Is the salmon any good?"

"I don't know. I never ate here before."

"Are you going to have a beer?"

"I was thinking of something stronger."

"This early in the day?"

"It's been that kind of week."

"It's only Monday."

"That's what I mean, Jo. Why haven't you finished the painting? You said it would be done over the weekend."

"What's the rush? I do have a thing called a job, you know. I can't just sit around the house all day like you."

"I work from my house."

"You'd probably get more accomplished if you rented an office outside your home, Trace. Have you ever thought about that?"

"Who says I'm not getting things accomplished?"

"You do. You say it all the time. You're always bitching about some deadline that's looming."

"That's the nature of my business. There's always a deadline and then another after that and another after that and on and on and on. I'll probably be writing something on deadline the day that I die. When're you going to finish the painting?"

"Stop it! Honestly. It's just a stupid painting."

"I can sell it for you. I want to sell it for you."

"Oh, I – "

"Don't make that face."

"I don't want you selling my paintings to your friends."

"Why?"

"I don't like your friends."

"Nobody likes my friends. I don't like my friends. They're movie people. They're totally unlikable. And if I tell them that something is art then they believe it's art because I'm smarter than them and they know it. I can make you into an artist, not that you aren't already one, but I mean an artist whose paintings sell."

"Oh, God. You're just trying to get back into bed with me. That's what this is all about."

"Not true, Jo."

"Yes, it is."

"No, it's not. I've met someone. We're dating."

"Really? Who?"

"I'm not saying. No one you know anyway."

"Is it that bitch you were fucking behind my back?"

"Jesus. Do you have to put it that way?"

"It is her. I'm certain. I know you."

"Really?"

"Oh, yeah."

"You didn't even know I like fish."

Trace at the Tam

The three hotel clerks continued to purr and cluck and banter back and forth about some billing process or other form of official business that had them in animated disagreement.

Trace knew he wasn't invisible to their gaze. They just figured he could wait, like all of the other Extended Stay guests. The bag of groceries was straining his grip. He could feel his fingers locking up from the psoriatic arthritis that had invaded his joints, as it always did during severe psoriasis flare-ups. Beneath the black leather glove that cloaked his hand the skin was dry and cracked and bleeding.

One of the hotel clerks clucked but not at Trace. "That's not the way I was taught to do it. You're supposed to hit the enter key and then – "

Trace gripped the alabaster handle on his walking stick and hobbled closer to the counter.

"Excuse me, ladies. Does it take three of you to have this conversation?"

One of the clerks, a pretty Chinese-American girl who, Trace noticed, sported one of those annoying plastic friendship bracelets on her left wrist, looked up and blinked demurely.

"Would you like your mail?"

"Yes. That's why I'm here."

"You don't have any."

"Are you sure?"

"Uh, huh. I just finished sorting it."

Trace could feel her eyes on his back as he limped toward the bank of elevators. On days when his psoriatic flare-ups were at their worst his public image was markedly different from other days: black leather gloves (one of the hotel clerks gratingly called them Trace's "O.J. gloves"), walking stick, dark sunglasses, and, when imposed upon, a gaze that threatened more violence than a Category Six Hurricane striking an island of grass huts.

No mail meant no paycheck yet. But he still had money in the bank, even after springing for lunch and cocktails that afternoon at the Tam O'Shanter Inn with one of his favorite local writers and the writer's webmaster.

Just over the hill from Los Feliz in Atwater Village, the Tam O'Shanter was – and still remains – one of L.A.'s finest gray ladies. A proclamation from Councilwoman Jackie Goldberg that hangs on the Tam's foyer wall says it all: "The oldest restaurant in Los Angeles in the same location under the same ownership and management."

When the restaurant was built in 1922, co-owner Lawrence Frank said that he wanted the eatery "to look like something from Old Normandy." When that design failed to click with patrons of the restaurant on the small country road that connected Glendale to Hollywood a friend of the owners made a suggestion.

"Why don't you call it the Tam O'Shanter after Robert Burns' famous poem?" he offered. "And you can put the waitresses in plaid costumes to carry out the idea."

And so it remains. Waitresses clad in plaid, Yorkshire pudding, and hearty roast beef sandwiches prepared from the previous day's cut of prime rib.

But Trace didn't eat at the Tam that afternoon. When he was on the healing side of a psoriasis flare-up – paradoxically, the most painful phase – he didn't have much of an appetite. He instead sipped three Bass Ales on tap and enjoyed the conversation with his friends.

After lunch, Trace took a Yellow Cab to a drug store near the hotel. He bought a sixteen-ounce bottle of dry skin therapy lotion for his hands and legs. He had not hydrated his legs all day, which meant that when he got home they would be cracked and bloody and in need of immediate attention.

By the time he got to the hotel desk to pick up his mail he was glad he had brought the walking stick along because he could feel the plaque psoriasis sores breaking open on the soles of his afflicted feet. The walk from the drug store to the hotel was enough to accomplish that bit of nastiness.

At the elevator Trace leaned on his cane for support. Every joint in his body was swelling from the arthritis. His skin felt like it was being treated with flaming sandpaper applied by a bear's claw.

Five more minutes, he told himself. Don't scream out loud. The elevator will be here and then you will be back in your room. Five more minutes. Hang in there, cowboy.

In the elevator an elderly Armenian man with white hair flowing out of his ears joined Trace, followed closely by a younger Armenian man cradling a toy black poodle in his arms.

"What happen?" the old man asked Trace, nodding to the walking stick, the only thing now holding him erect.

"Lots of things, arthritis, nerve damage."

"Nerve damage?" There was a hint of German in the old Armenian's accent. "From car? Accident?"

"No. From scratching, damage I did from scratching too hard with things I should never have scratched with." He smiled. "I have a skin disease."

The old man waved a finger at Trace's gloved hands.

"And?"

"That's part of the skin disease. Psoriasis."

The old man's face clouded over. Trace knew that would throw him. The young man then exchanged explanatory words with the old man.

"Mutti," the young man said, and made a sweeping gesture over the flesh of one arm. *Mutti.* German for "mommy." He knew he caught a Germanic lilt in the old man's voice. In his daily travels around Glendale, Trace noticed that Armenians spoke a fascinating language peppered with words and phrases in French, German, and Russian.

"Mutti," the old man repeated and nodded his head sympathetically.

The doors slid open and Trace stepped out of the elevator car with a nod and half-smile to both men. The young man held up the black poodle as if the dog, too, bade Trace well.

"I fucking hate poodles," Trace said under his breath as the tip of his cane hit the carpet and he hobbled like a crooked man down the long hallway.

Endings

Trace poured a second cup of morning coffee and read the last four sentences of the e-mail again.

"I wish you the best of luck. I don't think you are a monster, you're just having a very difficult time, but you have lots of people around you now that care. We are all done here. Goodbye, Trace."

He lit a cigarette and listened to the children playing in the schoolyard across the street, the soundtrack to his life five days a week. That and CNN droning in the background on the hotel TV. He loved white noise, thrived on it.

We are all done here, she wrote.

Trace glanced at the book pitch he composed the night before for a friend. Not bad. He hoped John would sell the book for a cool million. The concept was good enough, he thought, and even had the smell of franchise all over it.

He snubbed the cigarette out in the round red ashtray on his desk. George Clooney smiled up at him from the cover of the latest issue of *Los Angeles* magazine.

We are all done here.

Well, he thought, at least I have something to write about this morning.

We are all done here.

Quick. Efficient. Bloodless. And totally unexpected.

It sounded like something that he would say.

Dead Man

"I was murdered," the man suddenly announced to Trace. "Killed. Right here in this hotel."

Trace studied the man's face in the mirror behind the bar. Thirty-five years old, he figured, going on fifty-five. Dark, unkempt hair and deep-set dark eyes encircled by the black rings of sleeplessness. Shabby, loose-fitting clothes. Fingernails bitten down almost to the cuticles. His hands were restless, fingers tearing at the edges of the cocktail napkin.

"What do you mean by that?" Trace said, knocking back a shot of blackberry brandy and taking a sip of the beer chaser.

"Give me a minute." The man pressed a thumb and index finger against his eye sockets, as if rubbing away sleep or a bad dream.

Moments before Trace had been lost in abstract thought about the women in his life. Why is it, he wondered, that the women who professed love for him wanted nothing further to do with him after the romance perished? Gina, the mother of his only child, refused to speak to him under any condition. And then there was Josephine. Trace and Josephine were married six years but in the last two years she had been back and forth between L.A. and the Bay Area as she tended to her father's dying days. Trace knew a split was inevitable. Josephine would be absent for two or three month stretches at a time, returning for a brief week or two to a man who was growing increasingly comfortable with the concept of living alone.

Trace tried to remain friends with Jo after the break-up but when he leaned on her for emotional support she folded like a freeway overpass in a major ground shaker. Lisa – his recent fling –

sympathized with Josephine when she told Trace that she no longer desired communication with him.

"Josephine loves you very much," Lisa explained, "but you shit all over her with your Dan Knight stories." After reading a recent story on Trace's website one evening, Lisa had vowed to disappear too if he ever dated another woman.

The man twisted in his bar stool and looked at Trace directly.

"I sought you out," he said.

"I beg your pardon?" Trace summoned the bartender for another beer.

"You're a writer."

"How do you know that?" Trace asked warily. "I don't believe we've ever met."

"I asked at the front desk."

"Why would you be interested in what I do for a living?"

The last thing Trace wanted was another stalker in his life.

"Well, no, I asked, like, in general if there were any writers living in the hotel. You figure in a residential hotel this big in L.A. there's gotta be at least a few, right?"

"Do you need a writer for something?"

"I just think you would be interested in my story. Somebody has to write it. You could make a lot of money with this story. Serious money, man."

One dollar for every time he heard that pitch would have bought Trace a great many things lacking in his life.

Trace sipped his beer and watched the man as he continued to tear tiny triangles off the edges of the cocktail napkin with his nervous fingers. Those restless hands reminded him of his friend Amy; her hands were small and delicate and whenever she and Trace were together those hands were in constant motion, as if they had a life of their own. They would rest in her lap momentarily only to abruptly appear on the table or the arm of the chair and then they would duck back into her lap again, the fingers always twitching and crawling and moving. She was a writer, too, a dedicated and passionate one, so Trace figured that her hands were always striking a keyboard even when she wasn't in physical proximity to one.

"Yeah, well, everyone has a story," Trace said, draining the last of his beer.

"I already gave you the opening line. What I said to you a minute ago. I was murdered. Killed. Right here in this hotel. Isn't that a killer opening? And that's what's gonna happen, man. Some people, some really fucked up people, are coming to kill me."

"Then hide. Get out of the hotel."

"I can't. They're watching me." He cast a furtive glance to the door to reinforce his drama.

"Uh, huh."

"Look, I can't talk here. But you have to hear my story, man. What's your name?"

"Trace."

"Trace. That's interesting. First name or last?"

Trace smiled. "Trace is all you need to know."

"Let me buy you a beer, Trace." He caught the bartender's attention and pointed a finger at Trace's empty beer glass. "Are you drinking to anything in particular tonight?"

The man's mind was wandering. A sure indicator, Trace thought, of ample drug use, probably meth. If there are killers stalking you, what does it matter what the man on the bar stool next to you is drinking to?

"To Darren McGavin," Trace said, "that's who I'm drinking to."

"The actor guy who died?"

"Yeah, that's him."

"Listen, like I said, I can't talk here. But, man, Trace, you have to hear my story, man. It'll blow your mind. If you want to come up to my room, I have some tina and – "

There it was. Tina, slang for crystal meth, which meant the man's fears were either very real or very, very imagined.

"I don't do meth," Trace interrupted. He glanced at the clock over the bar. "And I have to get back to work anyway."

Trace slid off the barstool.

"Burning the midnight oil, huh?"

"Always."

The fact of the matter was that Trace preferred to write in the evening. His desk was situated next to the sliding glass door of his hotel room, which afforded a sparkling view of the downtown L.A. skyline.

"Maybe I'll see you around, Trace?"

"Maybe."

"Don't forget my opening line," he said with a lopsided grin as Trace started out of the bar.

I was murdered. Killed. Right here in this hotel.

The words did indeed stay with Trace as he walked to the elevator. He thought of the man's restless hands clawing away at that napkin.

Punching the elevator button for the fifth floor, Trace's mind flashed on Amy's hands and he wondered if they were hovered over a keyboard right now, making words come to life on the blank page, or if they were beneath the soft sheets of her bed, anxiously twisting as she slept.

Running

"How many miles do you jog every day?" Trace asked.

"I don't know. I don't care about keeping track of things like that. I drive up to the Hollywood Reservoir and I do about seven or eight laps. I guess it's a few miles at least."

"Hard asphalt?"

"What?"

"The jogging trail, isn't it hard asphalt? I mean, that has to be bad on your shins and tendons, right?"

"I stretch first."

"Ah. Do you eat before or after?"

"After. Running gives me a big appetite."

"Why?"

"Huh?"

"What's the point? I mean, you know what happened to Jim Fix, right?"

"No. Who's Jim Fix?"

"Big jogging guru in the Seventies and Eighties, helped introduce granola to an unwitting public. Died of a massive heart attack while running."

"That's funny you say that as you light a cigarette."

"I don't lay claim to a healthy lifestyle but I try."

"Smoking and drinking?"

"I don't drink as much as I once did," Trace said. "Can't, not with the antidepressants."

"With the right diet and exercise you wouldn't need antidepressants."

"I'm not so sure about that. Here's my card. Call me sometime soon if you're in the mood. I'm writing an article about L.A. joggers and marathoners and I'd love to interview you. We can meet for coffee or something."

"I don't drink coffee."

"Okay, a drink then or – "

"I don't drink either. Actually, I live a pretty simple and basic life. I do my run in the morning, go to work, come home and get ready for the next day. I don't even own a television."

"Christ," Trace hissed. "Do you have a pulse or is that the point of the morning run?"

ACT TWO:
July – December 2005

Clowns

Trace didn't particularly care about clowns one way or the other but he liked Amy because she was also a good writer.

"The problem with clowns in a contemporary context," Trace told Amy, "is that they've been culturally marginalized, which is to say that the whole carnival and circus experience of our youth has also been marginalized and forgotten."

He took another sip of his second glass of Molson Ale to clear his dry throat.

"Hell," he said, "the circus experience today is all about dozens of Lipizzaner stallions with Frenchmen in black tights dancing on their backs."

Amy had asked Trace about coulrophpobia, the clinical name for fear of clowns, and he had gone off on a tangent. He signaled the bartender for another beer and regrouped his thoughts.

"People are afraid of clowns because their true emotions are concealed behind that painted-on smile and big red nose," Trace said.

"And then there's John Wayne Gacy," Amy offered.

"Indeed," Trace replied. "Here – "

He reached into his briefcase and extracted a manila folder containing a few notes he had collected for Amy on clown phobia. Just for kicks, he also brought her two DC comic books and one graphic novel, featuring Batman in battle against The Joker.

It was a dry afternoon. Trace and Amy had agreed to meet at Jax Bar and Grill in the center of the Glendale Business District for drinks, a little socializing, and, more importantly, for Trace to act as a sounding board for the new book that Amy was writing, a roman à clef about her experiences as a birthday party clown for the children of L.A.'s rich and famous.

Trace had arrived for the 12:30 meeting at noon, aware that by 12:30 the bar and tables and booths at Jax – famous for its nightly jazz seven days a week – would be overflowing with smart young men and women in their pressed suits, the legions that swarmed out of the high rises and onto the city sidewalks to prowl for lunch. By two o'clock the buildings would swallow them up again and downtown Glendale would be returned to the Armenian populace.

He grabbed a stool at the bar, laid his briefcase across the next stool to hold it for Amy, and ordered a Molson on tap from the attractive young bartender. She had shoulder length blonde hair and the nametag that was attached to the white shirt at her left breast said her name was Kirsten.

The beer was good. He hadn't eaten anything all day and probably wouldn't eat when Amy arrived unless she insisted on it. Psoriasis and its accompanying ailments left him with little or no appetite during the day. Only at night, while under the influence of a bowl or two, would his appetite rear its head.

As the bar began to fill up with suits and skirts and people with healthy skin and wide toothy smiles Trace sipped his beer and leafed through the research he brought for Amy. He thought briefly about a woman he loved once who was a guest on the *Bozo the Clown* television show in the 1960s when she was a child. She went to the taping convinced she was going to win one of the Schwinn bicycles that Bozo gave away every so often. When she was sent home without a shiny new bike she seethed and burned and developed a hatred of Bozo the Clown that lingered well into her mature years. In fact, Trace was convinced she would go to her grave with the reassurance that in death her thoughts would never again be plagued by images of Bozo the Clown, the Great Bicycle Cheater.

Trace returned the research notes to the manila folder. That's when he noticed that he was bleeding. There was a small crimson stain on the folder near the tab. He examined his hands in the dim light of the bar. There was blood all over his left index and middle finger. His right hand was similarly stained with blood.

Shit, he thought, I'm bleeding.

It was an old psoriatic joke: A man walks up to a psoriasis patient and says, "Excuse me, do you know you're bleeding?" The sufferer smiles and says, "Of course. Can you be more specific, please?"

The bar was now Standing Room Only. Amy wasn't due for another five minutes and Trace needed to get to the bathroom and stop the bleeding from wherever it was coming, probably somewhere on his face, a deep scratch from a pitted and deformed fingernail. But he couldn't leave. Someone would swipe their stools.

Trace was relieved when Amy arrived at 12:30 on the nose. The first time he'd seen her was on the dust cover of one of her books – she was, among other things such as wife and mother and part-time college instructor, an accomplished author of mystery novels. Trace thought she was cute, a wry little pixie on a slender frame with dark eyes, curly dark hair, and a hint of mischief about her that he couldn't identify. He wondered what she looked like in clown garb.

"Excuse me, Wags," Trace stood as she took a seat at the bar. He always called her by her clown name. "I'm bleeding from somewhere and I have to go see what it's all about."

Amy smiled, nodded, and ordered coffee.

"We're drinking alone today," Trace muttered to himself as he leaned on his cane and fought his way through suits and skirts to the small men's room at the back of the restaurant. It was rare for him to drink in the afternoon, anyway, except in social situations. Amy couldn't drink that day, Trace knew, because she had to take her daughter to the orthodontist that afternoon. No one wants to be around an inebriated clown-novelist-mother-wife-college instructor, particularly not orthodontists.

One quick glance in the dirty bathroom mirror and Trace saw the source of the blood. A scratch on the bridge of his nose was oozing pustules of blood. Trace staunched the flow with a handful of tissue he fished out of his suit coat and considered the delicious irony with a soft chuckle.

Trash

"The movie is an all-around piece of crap," Trace told his friend. "If you were paid for directing it you should be ashamed of yourself."

"You have to fix it for me."

Trace laughed long and hard into the telephone handset. "Do you have any idea how bad it is?"

"Fuck you. I know that," Norman growled. "I asked if you can fix it."

"Why would you want to change anything? It is what it is, a bad gonzo movie."

Norman began badgering his old friend, a technique that usually worked after Trace had his requisite temper tantrum.

"C'mon, Trace, it'll take you all of fifteen minutes and you'll earn a quick four hundred dollars."

Trace took a deep breath and silently counted to five before answering.

"Do you know what they say about a sow's ear and a silk purse?"

"I don't want to turn it into a silk purse. I just want it to be better!"

"It can't be better, Norman. The movie is garbage. The whole genre is garbage. Look, there's a reason I was never associated with these kind of movies when I was writing porn."

"Oh, bullshit," Norman shot back, "you wrote gonzo."

"Okay. Fine. I did. But you can count on one hand how many I did. And they were very theme-specific. This movie isn't."

"It's anal!" Norman shouted over the line.

"That's not a theme. It's an orifice."

Norman knew Trace would concede. After ten more minutes of debate, the lure of the quick payday compelled Trace to take the job.

After writing more than two hundred screenplays for adult films and videos in the Nineties, the field was as stale and moldy to him as a two-week-old loaf of bread. He had no fresh ideas for porn.

Trace slid the VHS screener of the rough cut of *Anal Exxxplosion* into the VCR and watched once more in horror.

"They're both butt ugly!" Trace had complained to Norman over the phone about the two porn stars selected to host the wrap-around segments that were sandwiched between the sex scenes.

"Yes, but they're two of the hottest girls in the business right now."

"You're kidding me," Trace said slowly. "Jesus Christ. What happened to the ones who actually looked like models?"

"That's so Nineties," Norman replied.

It was the wrap-arounds that needed repair. The actresses had flubbed their dialogue repeatedly and somehow forgot to look into the camera during most of their line recitals. It reminded Trace of watching a hostage video on CNN. The girls had that same furtive sideways glance thing going on.

Norman had given Trace a two-day deadline. By the eleventh hour of the second day he still had not written a word. He spent an hour on the phone with Norman trying to convince him to simply release the movie as it was.

"It's gonzo," Trace complained. "Who's going to notice whether the wrap-arounds are good or bad?"

"The cable companies will," Norman said. "I need a cable sale."

With forty-five minutes remaining in the eleventh hour, Trace tired of staring at the keyboard and tried some avoidance techniques to limber up his creative capacity. He washed his dishes in the hotel bathtub. He grabbed a plastic trash bag and began collecting the garbage neatly piled in a corner in smaller plastic trash bags.

Thirty minutes remaining before the deadline and Trace was toting the trash bag down the hotel hallway. He was less than four feet away from the plastic garbage bin when the bag inexplicably broke open and regurgitated its contents onto the carpet. He stood there in stunned disbelief amid a trash heap of wet coffee grounds, empty beer cans and a wine bottle, cigarette butts, hamburger wrappers from various fast food joints.

"For fuck sake!" he shouted. As he ducked down the adjoining hallway that led to back to his room, Trace saw a man and woman toting luggage down the hallway. They paused to consider the pile of offensive garbage in their path.

"I told you this place was a dump," the man told the woman.

Back in his room, Trace flattened the cardboard wrapper from a Budweiser twelve-pack and raced back down the hall. He used the Bud box as a dustpan and scooped every last beer can and cigarette butt into the trashcan. The pile of coffee grounds he left for the housekeeping staff to contend with.

In the fifteen minutes remaining on his deadline Trace sat down and pounded out a five-page script without thinking.

"Monkeys and typewriters," he muttered as he hit the send button to e-mail the script to Norman.

Corned Beef Hash and Eggs

A small gold tie clip held the simple black tie flat against the white Polyester dress shirt. His sleeves were rolled to the elbow but there was no sports coat or blazer draped around the back of his chair.

He must have left it at the office, Trace thought, sizing up the man as he approached the table.

The diner was a handsome young business type. Total business. This man knew nothing of the street, not a whisper, which was probably why he flinched when he looked up from his salad and saw Trace gazing at him.

Chicken shit, Trace said to himself.

The waitress led Trace to his own table opposite the young man's. What had caught Trace's eye in the first place was the young man's lunch companion. She was perhaps thirty years old and was simply stunning in her beauty. Her soft brown eyes were almond-shaped and her shoulder length hair was a shade of brown in perfect symmetry with her eyes. There was a hint of an olive complexion to her lustrous skin. Trace supposed that she was of mixed Latin and Hispanic pedigree. She wore a pink cotton blouse that hung loose on her lean frame. Her knee-length skirt was a simple white. A pair of very worn black stiletto heels finished off the outfit.

Trace ordered an iced tea and fumbled with the menu. He didn't need to look at it. He always ordered the same thing when he ate at Foxy's Café.

"Corned beef hash and eggs," he told the waitress. "Eggs over easy, hash browns well-done, and sourdough for toast."

Foxy's had toasters at the table for patrons to prepare their own bread, like the old Tiny Naylor's franchise once had. Trace never understood the gimmick but he liked it nonetheless.

He settled into his chair, added sugar and lemon to his tea, careful not to get any lemon juice into the cracked skin on his hands, and quietly studied the young man and woman across from him.

The young man spoke excitedly and with great passion. The woman held onto his every word with almost religious zealousness. She would stare into his eyes for minutes on end while he spoke between forkfuls of salad. He was animated and intense. And all he talked about was business.

Trace picked up stray bits of dialogue here and there between lulls in the restaurant white noise. The young man was clearly her boss or supervisor. The company was really going places in the years ahead. He had plans, yes indeed, he had plans and he was very serious about them.

But what made the tableau so fascinating for Trace to observe was that woman, that beautiful goddess with a small birthmark on the left side of her chin and another one further down on her silken throat. Trace doubted that the young man lunching with the woman noticed any of these things about her. He was all business. Total business.

It wasn't until fifteen minutes after sitting down, when his food finally arrived, that Trace even heard the woman speak. Her voice was disappointing, the kind of squeak one would associate with an airhead blonde, but she was mercifully short on words because her dining companion just rolled right over her with whatever bit of inanity he had to contribute next.

The woman listened to him as if he was speaking in tongues that only she understood. She studied his body approvingly when his eyes strayed away from hers. She was, clear and simple, smitten with her co-worker. And he, the potential object of her amorous affections, was completely eyeless to the whole thing.

Does it really matter? Trace asked himself as he paid the bill. A woman that intensely set on a man, he knew, would find a way to have him come hell or high water.

Unless, Trace thought, the guy was gay. That would explain a lot.

A Sexual Obsession with Soup Pots

When Trace developed arthritis and carpal tunnel syndrome from fifteen years of slamming away at typewriters and keyboards he traded in his old handgun for a System Automatic 9mm revolver with an ergonomic grip.

"Why do you have a gun?" Lisa asked. She wrapped the soft, brown sheets around her bare breasts and sat up in bed to light a cigarette.

"I was trying to figure out a way to tell you this," he sighed. They had been dating for a few months and Lisa was still eagerly learning Trace's secrets. "Sometimes I get stalkers in my life."

"Stalkers?" She didn't know whether or not to take him seriously. He was marginally successful as a writer but as a public figure he was all over the map. If a movie star that Trace once wrote a screenplay for made a major public statement, Trace would feed his own press release into the normal channels of distribution either supporting or denouncing the actor.

"Anything to keep my name out there in the public eye," Trace explained to Lisa.

Being in the harsh neon glare of public scrutiny, Trace told her, can attract an awful lot of lunatic moths. Lisa smoked her European cigarette in bed while Trace extracted a thick file from a desk drawer.

"This one is a fan. She bought my book and began sending me normal e-mails, or what seemed normal at the time. Just 'loved this chapter, didn't like this chapter' kind of shit and then three days after Hunter Thompson bought the enchilada, she sent me this – "

Trace pulled a printed e-mail out of the folder and read aloud: "When the mystics kill themselves, it's a sure sign. Trace, are you a viable sperm donor? I have the desire to become pregnant with the soul of Hunter S. Thompson."

Lisa fell back on the bed in a paroxysm of laughter.

"What?" Trace regarded her with a half-smile. "It's not that funny. It's kind of flattering to be compared to Thompson. I learned a lot from his work."

"I guess you learned better than you know," Lisa teased.

Trace moved to the side of the bed, kissed her on her bare shoulder, returned to the desk and the file. He pulled out two sheets of paper stapled together. "This one arrived a couple of nights ago."

"Dear Trace," he read aloud. "I'm at the library after just visiting my friend Jack at his studio. I listen quietly outside his door as he maliciously flirts with the middle-aged moms of his students. We went and had coffee and we're good enough friends that we get a kick out of recreating the conversations. He told me today that he cried when John Wayne died.

"I guess I'm at a turning point in the story I've been writing. I'd like to fill you in, because it literally writes itself every day. I am the obsession of my friend Trevor who is a prisoner of his own mind. He is truly brain-damaged from brain surgery performed courtesy of the U.S. government while he was incarcerated. He moves porn. I know Trevor like the back of my hand.

"Trevor developed some nontraditional methods of getting off long ago when his dad was a mill-rat working and abusing his twin sons in Gary, Indiana, the same mill that another man I know is a prisoner of. The other man is a prisoner of the mill's secrets and is a very wealthy religious man. He is also obsessed with me. He is a safe person. We are friends. We don't have sex, I am just a compassionate listener of the woes he has in his misguided marriage. Besides he's not my type. Neither is Jack, but anyway. The two men don't know each other."

Trace paused as he turned to the next page.

"Are you following so far?" he asked Lisa.

"I – I think so."

"Cool. So, continuing then – "

Trace read aloud:

"One of Trevor's only three ways of getting off is by bashing in the heads of crack whores when fucked up while he's fucking them. Sometimes he gets carried away and a missing person is one that no one would miss. Another form of satisfaction is his creation of homemade soups and chilies and he has a sexual obsession with soup pots. When he was in prison, he prided himself on developing recipes and creating soups out of almost nothing. 'It's the spices.' He was honored to be trusted in the prison kitchen 'with the knives!!' Trevor is not the first cannibal I've met.

"I've had a good relationship with Trevor, until today. He phoned me from Florida, he's on his way back and he's flipped. I never told him not to call me anymore and I did today and the side of Trevor reserved for his victims, well that's rearing its ugly head and it is his obsession with my daughter that leads him to his obsession with me and he let me know today, that there is NOTHING that will stop him from making soup in my Williams Sonoma stock pot in my kitchen.

"On my way to the states attorney I am in the a.m. because I now know I must, must get a restraining order against him and when he finds this out I don't know what's going to happen because he depends on me, and knows I'm privy to his secrets. I pray for the victims along the way. He has an interstate route and calls me with his whereabouts. I have tried to go to the police before but they don't care, as he's not wasting anybody of any importance.

"I wish, Trace, that you would call me, but I really don't know what I'd say. Maybe you could listen to me cry. The only lies that matter are the ones you tell yourself, and if you believe them, there is truly a problem.

"The dichotomy of being the obsession of two men, both victims of the mill, the sad steel industry of Gary, the birthplace of Michael Jackson. I believe this is interesting reading. Say, Trace, if I die soon I hope you can use some of this stuff for a new screenplay or somethin'. Pray for me. I pray for you. I love you, guy."

Trace returned the e-mail to the folder.

"Holy shit!" Lisa blurted. "Call her? Do you have this nut's phone number?"

"She called me once and left a message," Trace mumbled, lighting a cigarette. "She wanted to know if I ever thought about creating a men's magazine for Christians. I think she called it *Porn For Christians.*"

"How the hell did she get your phone number?"

"It's on my press releases."

"You have got to change that."

"So I'm told."

"Did you show that e-mail to a professional?" Lisa asked.

"Well, that's not the end of it but, yeah, a friend of mine who works in clinical psychology took a look and said that it was best to ignore her – that is, until the next e-mail came in."

Trace extracted another sheet from the folder and read to Lisa:

"I'm at Satan's house – do not reply. I read your most recent stories and, damn, you scare me sometimes. I was looking in the mirror the other day after brushing my teeth and thinking there is no way I could possibly attend the academy awards because I refuse to wear a gown and I have not had a facelift or Botox or anything and I was looking at how except for the double chin I don't need it but I was stretching my neck and decided that the reason my throat is not firmed is because I have not been exercising my throat muscles in deep throat fashion. I used to have a daily blowjob routine, and I didn't realize that, that, kept my chin(s) firmed. I am so out of practice. Do you think it's like riding a bike?"

Trace stopped. "Here she makes a reference to one of my stories called 'Poor Sonofabitch' – the part about brown sheets and you – and when we get to the part about 'Son Of A Whore' that's also a reference to one of my pieces."

He continued reading:

"I have brown sheets too. They are not brown; they are taupe. Rhymes with dope. I wish I were Lisa. And then 'Son of a Whore.' You're the whore, Trace, you sell your soul, your stories, your brilliance. I am not a whore. I give my shit away for free. I just give my heart away for free too. I am a survivor, and you shouldn't talk about your son with such disrespect. I can say whatever I want, cuz I'm disturbed.

"I gotsta go. Oh p.s....I was hugging my black squishy heart pillow and holding you and I said you poor, poor man. God, please keep this man safe, his potence has not been realized (I think that was Thurs.)."

Trace returned the e-mail to the folder with all of the others and placed the file back in the drawer for safekeeping.

"She's also sent me gifts in the mail."

"Gifts?" Lisa asked incredulously. "She has your address, too?"

"It's on my press releases and my website."

Trace poured a shot of chilled Potter's Vodka into an "I Love L.A." shot glass and downed it in one throat-scorching gulp.

"So now you know why I own a gun. I promise you that not all the answers to simple questions about my life are this complex."

Lisa cocked her head and blinked her eyes.

Trace Couldn't Write

Trace couldn't write. It's not that he had writer's block. He didn't believe in any such mental malady. Learn the craft and discipline of writing, he once told a student, and you'll never be blocked.

"You'll have off days, sure," Trace had said. "But even the guy working the counter at 7-Eleven has off days. Do you think there's such a thing as 7-Eleven clerk block?"

So he most definitely did not have writer's block. He owed a story to a publisher but he just couldn't write it. Earlier in the day his friend Norman the porn director called and left a message on Trace's cell phone.

"I just met with Jay from Roman Pictures. He wants you to think of a *Body Heat*-style porn script. I know, I know, it's probably been done a million times but come up with a hook, a twist. And I got some other offers coming for you too."

No matter how many times Trace told Norman that he was out of the porn scribbling business for good there was always an offer coming in. Norman still tied his career in adult films to Trace's talents as a screenwriter. Norman's affiliation with Trace was often enough to seal a deal.

But Trace couldn't write. And he would have to put his foot down with Norman and say, "How many times have I told you I'm out? I'm having a hard enough time writing these days as it is. And my health isn't exactly in tip-top condition, you know. If you made a lot of people promises that I would write movies for you without consulting me first, well, don't blame me when I send you back to them with your ass in a hat."

That's what he would tell Norman, just as he had told him hundreds of times before. Yet every time Trace would concede after weeks of plaintive whining and write the damn script in thirty minutes, collect a quick paycheck, and hate himself for about two weeks and three days. But, in the end, he was helping his friend, always helping talent-challenged Norman.

Trace stared at the blank Word document. He couldn't write. Another mitigating factor might have been the fact that for the first time in fourteen years Trace was utterly and completely single. There were no women to complicate and otherwise fuck up his life. He liked that but he was still going through an odd period of adjustment.

His skin was bad – legs aflame with the red ravages of pustular psoriasis – and he was back walking with the cane again.

He hadn't written anything in days. He had an urge to write, an almost primal hunting instinct, and he had the further motivation of a paycheck in the future, but he just couldn't write.

Trace poured another beer, took another hit off the pipe, and stared at CNN on the TV for a beat. They were reading the letter left behind by a dead West Virginia coal miner.

He returned to the desk and addressed the keyboard and began writing:

"I can't write. It's not that I have writer's block. I don't believe in any such mental malady. Learn the craft and discipline of writing, I once told a student, and you'll never be blocked."

A Ghost Story

"Write a ghost story," Amy suggested.

"What?"

"Don't you normally write a short story on Sunday night? Write a ghost story tonight."

"I don't know any ghost stories," Trace protested.

The truth was he knew a lot of ghost stories; not the rattling chains and haunted houses and madwoman-in-the-attic sort of ghost stories but tales of spectral souls still walking the earth, the beaten-down who had died in spirit so long ago but whose bodies had refused to give up. Or sometimes it was something in their spirit itself that stubbornly neglected to surrender, either way these were the only ghosts he knew and he encountered them on a day-to-day basis.

They're all over L.A., Trace thought, the whole goddamn city being nothing but a subterranean cemetery for walking corpses and the restless spirits of those long dead for whom material wealth and glamour and fame wasn't enough; they still yearn for it beyond the grave, haunting the barren sound stages and the musty old hotels and bungalows with semen-saturated mattresses that were first laid on the Hide-A-Bed foundation in 1932 and dank bar rooms that smell of old wet newspapers and piss and warm beer and the once-swank restaurants where they once ruled the roost that were nothing more now than mere curiosity items awash in dim lighting and plush red booths and stale memories.

A quick and astute glimpse in the mirror behind the bar at Musso and Frank on Hollywood Boulevard, Trace reasoned, was enough to conjure up a legion of the long gone.

"I don't think I want to write a ghost story," Trace said.

"All right," Amy said softly, "then let's talk about something else."

"Spider Palm"
A Dan Knight Story

"It's a spider palm."

"What?"

"A spider palm," Dan repeated, nodding toward the potted plant to the right of the hotel's pneumatic glass doors. To Avery, the plant resembled his daughter's punked-out hair, all green and willowy and full of spikes.

"Did you know there're over twenty species of palm trees?"

"I had no goddamn idea." Avery frowned and fished a cigarette out of a crumpled pack of Marlboros. He hated buying cigarettes in the soft pack. There was always a renegade smoke that got stuck in the back as the pack began to empty.

"Palm trees don't belong here, you know. They've been planted over the decades by immigrants. Spaniards, Iraqis, Egyptians."

Avery craned his neck to see if the yellow-topped Crown Victoria sweeping into the hotel driveway was the cab they were waiting for. It wasn't, of course. Nothing in Avery's life ever arrived on time. He fired up the cigarette and blew a plume of smoke in Dan's direction.

"Can I have one?" Dan asked.

"I thought you quit."

Dan hiked his shoulders. Avery gently shook one loose from the pack and extended it to his friend.

"The date palm," Dan explained, sucking in a lungful of blissful smoke, "is mentioned in the Bible. Have you ever been to the bluffs overlooking the ocean in Santa Monica?"

"How the fuck is that possible? You know this is my first trip to L.A."

"There's so much to see here."

"Yeah, well, I'm not on a sight-seeing excursion," Avery growled. His patience, always thin even in the best of times, was being sorely tested. Once the cab arrived he knew that Dan would stop his incessant and inane chatter. Dan was always quiet in taxi-cabs because they scared the hell out of him ever since the incident in Kansas City.

"Palm trees are monocots, soft tissue plants. They're different from other trees, which are called dicots."

"Do tell."

"Dicots – normal trees, that is – produce secondary growth if a branch is injured. Not so with the monocot. Lose a branch if you're a monocot and you're pretty much fucked."

"Tough break."

"Oh, Jesus, Avery. I didn't mean it that way."

"I didn't take it that way, Dan."

Dan quietly nodded and sucked on his cigarette.

"Thousands of palm trees die every day. They need human intervention and care to keep the species going. They're not the most self-sustaining plant on the block."

Avery shot him a dead look just as the Yellow Cab swept into the driveway. Dan collected his luggage and extinguished the cigarette in the moist dirt engulfing the potted spider palm.

"If you have so much respect for palm trees," Avery remarked, "why the hell did you just toss your cigarette in there?"

"I didn't say I respect them or anything. I was just telling you something I read once."

Dan remained silent through the entire fifteen-minute drive to the funeral home in Culver City and he never spoke about palm trees again for the rest of his life.

Rockville on My Mind

Trace wanted to go to Rockville and get drunk at Fitzgerald's grave but Marcel wouldn't hear of it.

"The magazine doesn't have that kind of money," Marcel said.

"How much is it going to cost? Three hundred dollars? Four? I won't even need a hotel. I'll sleep on a park bench. Better yet, I'll sleep in the cemetery."

"Why do you want to do this?" Marcel asked. He was skimming Trace's latest contribution to the leftist journal *Kidnap*. It was an interview with anti-porn crusader Duke Sebastian that promised to be quite provocative.

"It would make a great story for *Kidnap*, Marcel."

"No, there's more to it than that." Marcel laid the article aside and slid his reading glasses off his face and clasped his hands on his desk like a benign psychiatrist confronting his patient head-on. "You're in a melancholy mood today."

"I'm in a morbid mood."

Trace reached to the floor for his canvas bag and rummaged around between the books and notepads and pens and assorted cell phones until he found the empty Altoids tin that held his joints.

"Morbid melancholy," Trace said, firing up a tightly rolled joint. "I think I'll use that as a title someday."

"You already did." Marcel smiled. "That trade magazine piece about people profiting from dead celebrities."

"Oh right." He took in a lungful of smoke and passed the joint to Marcel. "I forgot about that one. You're my biggest fan, aren't you, Marcel?"

"I keep up with your work," Marcel replied nonchalantly, bringing the joint to his thin lips. Trace noted that Marcel's fingers were always stained with indelible red ink from the Sharpee he wielded as an editors tool.

"Am I any good?"

"You're better than most."

Trace nodded thoughtfully. Better than most was acceptable.

"What's really going on, Trace? How's Leggy Lisa?"

"Lisa's great. I just want to go to Rockville and get – "

"Stop with this craziness about dancing on Fitzgerald's – "

"Not dancing. Drinking. Getting drunk. On Fitzgerald's grave. In Rockville, Maryland."

Marcel passed the joint across the desk.

"I met this guy in a bar on Hollywood Boulevard today," Trace started.

Marcel rolled his eyes.

"What? You can't meet interesting people in a bar, Marcel? Anyway, I stopped in for a beer and I had a copy of *Gatsby* with me."

"Do you always bring reading material to bars? Doesn't that inhibit the social process?"

"Quite the opposite, Marcel. It's a sure conversation starter. You need to get out more often. So, I'm sitting there having a Red Hook and leafing through *Gatsby*, trying to remember what it was old Owl Eyes says at Gatsby's funeral – "

"Poor sonofabitch," Marcel quoted from memory. "It was also what Dorothy Parker said when she viewed Fitzgerald's body."

"Uh, huh. So there's a guy sitting there, kind of a nondescript fellow, around thirty maybe, and we start talking about Fitzgerald and it turns out this guy went to Richard Montgomery High School, which is in Rockville, Maryland, right off a major road called Rockville Pike."

"Wasn't there a novel called *Rockville Pike?*"

"Yes, by Susan Coll. Am I going to get through this pitch without interruption? Christ, Marcel."

"I'm sorry, Trace. Go ahead."

Trace fumbled in his bag until he found his wire-bound memo book and leafed through it manically until he found the tattered pages carrying his hastily drawn notes.

"On one side of the pike there's the high school campus, this guy tells me. If you walk up the campus and cross the pike, there's a very small church on a very, very small hill." He checked his notes for a moment before proceeding. "To the left of the church there's a small graveyard on the hill. It's not protected by any gates or stone wall or anything. You can just walk up in it. All the gravestones are small, he tells me, except for one towards the back center. It towers above all the others, and that's Fitzgerald's. The headstone stands up in the traditional upside down U-shape, and then a slab of stone lays flat with an inscription from *Gatsby.* Scott and Zelda's names are on the headstone."

Trace lit the joint again and took another huge toke while studying his notes.

"Here's the thing, Marcel, here's the fucking story, okay? His creative writing teacher used to take the class to write by the stone sometimes when the weather was nice. He said all the kids that were into literature were fascinated to have his stone right there; so whenever they passed through the graveyard – which was pretty often, since the shortcut from the school to the subway station was directly through the graveyard – they would leave a token of esteem, a cigarette or a joint or sometimes they'd plan ahead and get him a bottle of something. He said they assumed other kids took them as they passed as needed, and left their own gifts when they could."

Marcel accepted the joint and stared at Trace blankly. "I'm sorry. I don't see the story here."

"What? Kids leaving joints and bottles of gin on Fitzgerald's headstone? You don't see the story?"

"What's really going on, Trace?"

Trace closed the notebook and slumped in the chair.

"Is everything okay with you? Things moved awfully fast with that divorce you know and sometimes – "

"Sometimes what? I'm forty-seven years old, Marcel. I know what I'm doing. I feel like I'm in love for the first time in my life and I'm excited and – "

He bit down on the remainder of the sentence.

"And what?"

Trace's breath caught in his chest for a moment. "I had to start clearing out the last of Josephine's stuff, she's picking it up tomorrow, you know. And I just don't…how, Marcel? I don't understand.

I need someone to explain to me how two people who presumably were in love with each other could be so toxic to each other. That question has been bothering me. What the fuck happens?"

"If I knew the answer to that question do you think I would be running a third-rate leftist journal from a loft in Long Beach?"

Trace reached for a cigar in his bag, lit it, and smiled at Marcel. "I suppose not. So, do you want to send me to Rockville?"

"Absolutely not."

"Shit." He took a long pull on the cigar. "Life really fucking sucks sometimes."

"If that's how you feel," Marcel smiled, "I won't tell you how it ends. You might not like it."

Intoxicate Me

"What am I going to do? Stage an intervention for the fucker? I don't know him well enough to care and he hasn't given me reason to give two shits about his marriage or his efforts to become a human ship in a bottle."

"I think he does want an intervention," Lisa told Trace. "Remember when he was writing on his website about his wife holding an intervention for her sister who was an alcoholic?"

"Yeah. That was a few months ago. So?"

"Isn't that when you said he suddenly started becoming morose and depressive?"

"Well, it was also a period when he started writing heavily about his drinking."

"Exactly!" Lisa practically shouted. "That's when he was writing all those lyrical stories about walking around Silverlake in search of a liquor store for his coveted Arrogant Bastard Ale."

Trace took a sip of his bourbon and water. "He was actually doing some good writing back then, in a Malcolm Lowry, *Under the Volcano* kind of way."

"With a lot of French influence."

"With a lot of French influence and who the fuck cares and we're getting away from the goddamn point, which is he leaves a rambling message on my website about how terrible his life is that he can't drink when he wants to because his wicked witch of a wife keeps tabs on every dollar that he spends and what for and, honestly, Lisa, I just think he's looking for an intervention, as you said."

"He's equating help with attention. He wants attention. He was jealous when the sister-in-law got an intervention."

"Yup. And if his wife read what he wrote at my website, the marriage would most definitely be over. Done. Kaput."

"He's the kind of drunk who has to lose everything and everyone before they quit and sometimes even then they don't."

Trace finished his drink and didn't order another. "I've got my own drinking under control. I don't have time to wet nurse another drunk. For chrissake, I grew up with them. Every one of my stepfathers was a lousy drunk."

"And you don't want to deal with them in your adult life."

"Nope."

Trace hoisted the remains of his bourbon and water and chewed on the dripping ice cubes at the bottom of the glass. He hoisted the empty glass in salute and recited from his favorite novel, *Miss Lonelyhearts*:

> Soul of Miss L, glorify me.
>
> Body of Miss L, nourish me
>
> Blood of Miss L, intoxicate me.
>
> Tears of Miss L, wash me.
>
> Oh good Miss L, excuse my plea,
>
> And hide me in your heart,
>
> And defend me from mine enemies.
>
> Help me, Miss L, help me, help me.
>
> In saecula saeculorum. Amen.

Trace gently placed his glass back on the bar. "And that's what I think about that."

"By the way, that was kind of funny."

"What was?"

"You didn't catch the humor in what you said a moment ago? You said he was writing heavily about his drinking."

"Oh. Shit."

Melville Blues

"It's *Moby Dick* with cops and robbers," Trace insisted.

Hovick leaned his bony elbows on the desktop and rubbed his chin thoughtfully. He was one of the youngest development executives in the movie business, rising from script analyst to administrative assistant to junior exec in less than a year and a half.

"Has there ever been a good movie made from *Moby Dick*?" Hovick mused.

"The John Huston version wasn't bad." Trace tossed back a long swallow from the twenty-ounce bottle of Aquafina in his quaking hands and screwed the cap back on before tossing it in the canvas bag at his feet.

"Never saw the Huston one. I saw the TV movie with what's-his-name, though."

"Patrick Stewart," Trace muttered. "I'll take Gregory Peck any day. But back to the script."

"Yes, please, back to the script."

Trace squirmed fitfully in the luxurious armchair at the side of Hovick's desk. Cheeky little bastard, he thought, twenty-three years old and he owns office furniture that's worth more than I'll ever have in the bank this year.

"It's the story of this female FBI agent whose sterling career is cut short when she encounters a notorious bank robber, attempts to perform an arrest, and he blows her leg off with a shotgun. That's the beginning of the movie. From there we cut to three years later and the woman has become a psychotic mess as a result of losing her job with the Bureau and she begins this crazed cross-country journey to find and kill the man responsible for ruining her life. And one more thing: because of losing her leg and all she's constantly on heavy duty painkillers, so she's a drugged-out psychopath with an expert marksmanship certificate from the FBI on an obsessive quest to seek revenge. See? It's just *Moby Dick* with cops and robbers, like I said."

Hovick sighed. "It's not a bad idea, Trace, but there's the literary pedigree to consider."

"What literary pedigree?" It took all of his self-control to prevent the words from leaping out as a bark and growl.

"You said *Moby Dick* with cops and robbers."

Now he did bark. "That was the pitch, Hovick! I didn't mean it too literally."

Hovick shook his head. "It's still going to be hard to get around with the studios. Everyone sees *Moby Dick* as a boring book. It's a joke on that level."

"Have you ever read it?" Trace growled. "It's actually quite good, you know. But I only used it for the pitch. You know, the hybrid. You guys like to hear that a script is a cross between this and that. The script isn't literally *Moby Dick*."

"But it is *Moby Dick*," Hovick persisted.

"No, I just use the paradigm of *Moby Dick* to tell the story. The chick is Ahab, the guy she's chasing is the big white whale, and the cops pursuing her sort of fill out collectively the role of Ishmael. They are the survivors, the ones who live to tell the story."

"Everyone is going to recognize the story as *Moby Dick* with cops and robbers, Trace, and they'll shy away from it."

"Why?" Trace said pleadingly.

"Because it's Moby-Fucking-Dick!"

"It is not." Trace set his jaw in a defiant pose.

Hovick withdrew a long breath that sounded like a balloon slowly losing its helium.

"Trace," he said in a measured tone, "you pitched it to me as *Moby Dick* with cops and robbers."

"The Kill Fee"
A Dan Knight Story

A blood red sun rises over the city. Helicopter blades scrape the smog-choked sky as news and police choppers scan the L.A. Basin for signs of trouble on the streets and freeways.

Dan Knight's vintage '48 Packard is snarled in northbound traffic on the Golden State Freeway. To the accompaniment of blaring horns, Dan bullies the car into the exit lane. He takes one hand off the wheel to pop open the glove compartment, where his .32 caliber Walther Semi-Automatic PPK rests within easy reach should any of the perturbed commuters decide to get frisky at his aggressive maneuvers.

"Asshole!" Dan hears an irate soccer mom shriek from her lime green SUV when he cuts her off in his desperate bid to make the Foothill Boulevard off-ramp.

Under normal circumstances, Dan wouldn't be caught dead in Tujunga, an eyesore of a city nestled between the Verdugo Hills and the San Gabriel Mountains. A K-Mart and a Denny's are the only branded establishments on Foothill Boulevard because the city's white trash citizenry keep most merchants at bay. Dan spies their faces on the sidewalks and in their battered Thunderbirds and pickup trucks: death merchant bikers, broken-down cowboys, welfare mothers, members of the Aryan Nation just itching to violate the terms of their parole.

But Dan Knight had a good reason to risk incurring road rage ….

Trace stopped typing.

"Risk incurring road rage?" he read aloud, a cigarette dangling from his lips. "What kind of alliteration is that?"

Trace blinked at the smoke curling up into his eyes and recalled something Lisa had said during their last date. "Do you have future plans for the Dan Knight stories – or are they just a … hobby?"

"Risk incurring road rage," Trace muttered again. He pounded the backspace button on the keyboard mercilessly until the offending phrase disappeared from the computer monitor. When the telephone rang he made no effort to comply with the summons. It could be David Dulce, the downtrodden gay hustler looking to make another quick celebrity slander sale to the tabloids. It might be Marcel DuPont, the editor of the leftist rag *Kidnap*, calling to offer Trace another quirky assignment, like the piece Trace just filed on the Taco Shop Poets.

"Cappuccino and poetry are no more!" the self-described cultural guerillas declared. "Long live salsa and the spoken word!"

The Taco Shop Poets were a group of Hispanic poets and musicians who routinely took over taco shops in San Diego, Tijuana, Los Angeles, San Francisco, Denver, New York, and beyond – "taking poetry to an audience not usually exposed to the spoken word and taking the usually jaded spoken word audience to a new environment for poetry."

"In other words," Marcel said when Trace first pitched him the story, "these clowns burst into urban taquerias and sing 'La Cucaracha' and spout poetry about Che Guevara."

"Well, it's a little more organized than that," Trace replied. "They're not staging daring Zorro-like raids and riding away on their trusty steeds."

Marcel only had to think for ten seconds before approving the story. "It's great. Take a photographer and get some pictures. We'll make it the cover story for the next issue."

It wasn't a call from Marcel that interrupted progress on the latest Dan Knight story, however.

"Trace, it's Jack Smalls," the message on the voice mail began. "I'm sitting in a car in Pasadena with Gray Hubler and we were wondering about the progress you were making with the *Super Villains In Prison* treatment. We're close by to you now if you want to hook up to discuss your progress. Give me a call. I'm on my cell."

Trace was glad he hadn't picked up the phone. He thought better of returning Jack's call directly so instead he dialed Jack's home phone number where he was assured to get an answering machine.

"Look, Jack, I have some issues we need to resolve before I can move forward with the treatment," Trace said with a cold snap in his voice when he reached the answering machine of Sally Port Films, the putative production company that Smalls ran from the living room of his modest Culver City home.

"You guys met with me several weeks ago. You pitched me a concept. We batted some thoughts around. I went home and spent two days writing a seventeen-page treatment only to have you guys turn it down for the most flimsy of reasons. Now you're asking me to write another treatment for free and what's my guarantee you won't reject this one as well? I need at least two fifty of the proposed five hundred upfront money for the script before I can move forward. It's only fair. You can't ask me to write two treatments for free."

He hung up without a closing salutation and tried to return to writing the new Dan Knight story. But within fifteen minutes the phone rang again and Caller ID pegged the nuisance as Jack Smalls.

"Hello, Jack," Trace said with dishonest pleasure in his voice.

"I got your message, Trace, and I've talked it over with Gray. He agrees with how you feel. And I agree with how you feel. So here's what we want to do: we want to give you a hundred for all the hard work you put in on the first treatment and proceed as already discussed on the next one: five hundred for the screenplay once we approve the treatment against seventy-five hundred dollars when we get the financing for the movie in place."

Trace found himself agreeing with their terms. A one hundred dollar kill fee was a joke. A blasphemous insult from a man he had known for twenty-seven years. But Trace had no intention of accepting the hundred dollars or writing the *Super Villains In Prison* treatment. He just wanted to see how low Jack Smalls would go.

"Fuck it," he said after he hung up. "Maybe I'll become a Taco Shop Poet instead."

He returned to his desk, lit a cigarette, and contemplated Dan Knight's new adventure.

Wilshire Boulevard

Trace craned his neck into the windshield of the car and gazed upwards at the rows of palm trees jutting into the night sky on a residential street off Wilshire Boulevard.

"I have an obsession with palm trees," he confessed.

"No shit," Amy said, eyes prowling for a parking spot. "I read your short story."

"Speaking of which," Trace said while marveling at the way the palm fronds were etched against a charcoal sky bordered by sodium light, "in that other story I wrote, the one about the bar room meeting, I didn't mean to use the word 'disappointed'."

Amy laughed. He turned to steal a glance at her face in laughter. Radiant, as always. How is it, he wondered, that someone so lovely can spend her life living under such a dark cloud?

"Anyway," Trace continued as she circled the Volvo around the block and headed back to Wilshire, "I meant that I was disappointed at the time that we hadn't planned the meeting for later in the day around two o'clock when the bar was less crowded."

"Ah," she said.

"The thing is, Wags, I'm a natural born people-watcher. When I'm in a crowded room no one has my complete attention. I'm always watching people and eavesdropping on conversations and, generally, as a writer, like you, too, I'm constantly observing."

"Uh, huh."

One more loop around the block produced a parking spot. When they settled into the plush red booth in the restaurant, she took one look around the room crowded with L.A. hipsters, lovely and creative and interesting people, and said, "Well, I guess there are a lot of people here for you to watch tonight."

The Rum Diary

The day began under a burnt orange sky. L.A. County had been under a red flag fire warning for two days and nature had finally complied, with high winds and extremely low humidity fueling a scorching brushfire in the Anaheim Hills south of Los Angeles.

Trace sipped his second cup of coffee and stood on his south-facing balcony, observing in wonder as the strong east-to-west Santa Ana winds sent choking plumes of smoke over the L.A. skyline. Thick fingers of smoke caressed the eastern slope of the Hollywood Hills at Los Feliz and Griffith Park.

Trace had three magazine features to prep that day and he had an infomercial to write for New Vibrations but everything would have to wait for another day. He felt disconnected and was in a considerable amount of pain.

"What am I going to do with all this shit?" Trace complained to his friend Norman, the porn director, when he arrived for their morning meeting with five cartons of freshly minted, perfectly packaged sex toys. "Did they really think I needed this much product to write an infomercial on how to sell vibrators? For Christ's sake."

Norman wore a serene smile and promised Trace that he would personally return any product that Trace didn't have a personal use for.

Trace launched himself out of his desk chair with the aid of his cane. He warmed his cold coffee in the microwave, lit a cigarette, and studied his friend for a beat. How long had Norman been shooting porn? Trace wondered. He had forgotten but he was sure that Norman started in the early 1980s, shortly after graduating from Emerson College with a degree in communications. Norman had his share of mainstream gigs in the past but the bulk of his income always came from shooting adult features – and not the high-end stuff. Not anymore.

"Look," Trace said. "I need this shit out of here sooner than later. What if I wanted to bring a lady back here some night?"

"Who?"

"Never mind who."

"So there is a 'who'." Norman folded his thick hands across his potbelly and flashed that serene smile again. He's stoned, Trace thought. A sixty-year-old stoner.

"If there is a who, it's no one you know, I can guarantee that."

"Oh? Then she's not a cheap slut? What happened to Lisa?"

"Well – " Trace was suddenly annoyed at Norman's probing questions. "Just get the stuff out of here. Soon."

"The faster you write the script, the faster I get the shit back to New Vibrations."

Norman was always pushing Trace to produce in record time. In the years when Trace was writing porn on a full-time basis it was not unthinkable for him to pound out a decent thirty-page script in a few hours. But he had moved on past porn scripts and triple X movie reviews and porn star interviews for skin mags years ago. He only ducked down the Porn Ghetto now as a means to a financial end.

"I'll get to it when I can get to it. Did you bring me anything for my depression?"

Norman always arrived bearing gifts, usually comps he picked up at conventions and almost always liquor because Norman didn't drink.

"Maybe." Norman reached into the bag at his feet and extracted a bottle of Castillo Silver Puerto Rican rum. But that wasn't all. There was an entire Piña Colada kit, complete with swizzle sticks and two shot glasses with palm trees painted on them.

"Sweet," Trace said. He put the bottle of rum on the wet bar and studied the directions for the Piña Colada. "Shit. You need a blender to make these. I don't have a fucking blender."

"So buy one, bonehead, they're only ten dollars."

Norman left only after extorting a promise from Trace that the script for the infomercial would be completed by the end of the week. Trace, as always, lied and said it would be done.

Trace spent the day glancing over the New Vibrations catalog and clawing through the cartons, pausing every so often to check on the progress of the fire in Anaheim. By two o'clock it had begun to rain ash in Glendale. Not heavy ash like L.A. gets when the fires are really raging, but certainly noticeable flakes of ash drifting from the sky.

By five o'clock Trace's mind was numb from looking at mechanical arousal devices. He wanted a Piña Colada. He wasn't in the mood to walk to Sears and buy a blender. The hotel bar wasn't open yet so he couldn't use José's blender.

And then he remembered the vacuum pump system.

Among the oddest novelties Trace was delivered was a large vacuum pump system. The notion behind this device was that the man inserts his penis into the end of a large two-and-one-quarter-inch clear cylinder and then works the high pressure vacuum pump with a set of padded handles (with an industrial grade pressure gauge attached) and supposedly the user, over time, would feel the benefits in lengthening and thickening of the member.

The vacuum pump was brand new, factory-sealed. Trace would never have a use for it. He was one of those rare men who was completely secure with his manhood.

"Never received anything but compliments," Trace always said.

Trace unwrapped the vacuum pump. There was more than enough room in that clear cylinder, he knew, to mix a Piña Colada and the vacuum pump would do the job of a blender just fine. But there was the matter of that open hole at the bottom of the cylinder, the opening for the penis. If he couldn't plug that up he would have Piña Colada all over the walls.

He hastily opened one of the boxes and found the shrink-wrap bag marked Anal Toys.

Perfect, he thought, a butt plug is fucking perfect.

Trace unwrapped the hard plastic butt plug and inserted it into the end of the cylinder. It was an easy and snug fit.

"Piña Coladas tonight," he sang as he limped to the wet bar.

The Misfits

It was a hazy September afternoon in Los Angeles. Trace sat in a hardwood deck chair in the backyard of the mansion, bored and listless as twenty-something porn starlets cavorted on the lawn of the four-acre backyard. There was a yellow pad in his lap and he scratched out a series of notes with his right hand while holding steady to his cane with his left hand.

The oddly disaffected voice of a young woman broke his languid concentration.

"I'll bet the handle of that cane perfectly matches your hand," the voice observed.

Trace slowly turned his gaze toward the girl who was standing at the edge of the deck chair. She stood before him as naked as the day she was born. The top and bottom of her damp sky blue bikini was clutched in her hand. She had long and lustrous red hair that cascaded down to her trim behind and a full and wispy bush of red pubic hair. Her legs were long and slender, her stomach, abs, and breasts as flat and tight as a young boy's. Trace figured her to be loitering in the vicinity of twenty-two years old.

"Let me see your hand," she said, taking Trace's hand into her own before he could say no. She held her own palm flat against his. "See? We have the same size hands."

She then reached for Trace's cane and spidered her palm across the artificial alabaster handle.

"Yep," she observed. "It's perfectly molded to fit your hand."

Trace waited for her to ask why he walked with the assistance of a cane – many people did, much to his amusement and annoyance –

but instead she simply abruptly ended the puzzling conversation and returned to the baronial estate.

The house was one of those faux colonial mansions in Encino, tucked away on a quiet side street north of Ventura Boulevard. It was, in fact, one of the originals from the 1930s when stars like Gable and Lombard built sprawling homes in what was then nothing but orange groves a stone's throw from Hollywood.

The owner of this house – a Georgian colonial – made a decent living renting out the home and the grounds to Hollywood studios and production companies for location filming. The movie that Trace was shooting that afternoon, a one-day affair, was a nightmarishly simple product for Pay Per View cable broadcast, an all-nude, one-hour special called *The Ultimate Spring Break Wet T-Shirt Contest.* The "contestants" were supposed to be college co-eds recruited from local campuses but they were in reality a clutch of young up-and-coming porn stars hired to play the part by Norman, Trace's director, co-producer and, sometimes, his best friend.

"It's *American Idol* with wet T-shirts," Trace concluded when he was hired to conceive, write and co-produce the show. The New York-based broadcaster only had four non-negotiable requirements, written over and over again in production memos to Trace and Norman: Lots of tits. Lots of nudity. Lots of wet T-shirts. Lots of fun. There was to be absolutely "no pink," meaning no photography of open orifices and no overtly sexual activity on-camera. Other than that, it was a walk in the park for very little money and even less prestige.

When it came time to shoot The Quick and the Wet Fast Draw Competition, Trace dragged his chair to the edge of the lawn where the filming was taking place. The concept was simple: Eight girls in flimsy T-shirts and little else squared off in groups of two for a gunfight with water-filled Super Soakers. Filmed in high-definition video by two cameras for full coverage.

Less than twenty seconds into the first round of competition, one of the young blue movie starlets slipped on the wet grass and came down with one slender leg making uncomfortable contact with a barbeque pit constructed of jagged stones. The immediate scene almost made Trace double over with laughter: naked porn stars sitting on the sidelines rushing out onto the grass to help their fallen comrade. It was a bad gash, to be sure, and all the production personnel scrambled to their grip trucks and personal vehicles for First Aid kits, the next best thing to non-existent Worker's Compensation in that shoddy industry where performers are only so much chattel.

"How are you feeling? Do you have anything to take?" Trace asked the injured participant fifteen minutes after the literal slip-up. She had hobbled to a deck chair next to Trace's, her leg expertly bandaged by one of the crew, and lit up one of Trace's cigarettes after asking permission.

"You mean do I have anything to take for the pain? Yeah, I have some Vicodin in my bag. I just need to rest first and then I'll go grab one."

Her name, Trace learned, was Leanna. He did not know if that was her real name or her porn moniker. Either way, it didn't matter to Trace. She appeared to be no older than nineteen, the professionally applied pancake make-up masking acne scars and a fresh crop of pimples erupting on her forehead. She was attractive as far as post-pubescent teens go, which made Trace momentarily consider what kind of waking nightmare it would be to get sexually and romantically involved with a girl that young and immature; after all, the girl sitting next to him was completely nude, save for the bandage on her gashed leg.

"I have all kinds of meds," she continued. "I have anti-depressants and anti-anxiety meds, all kinds of them. I have these really bad anxiety attacks. Have you ever had one?"

Trace laid his book aside. He had been reading A.C. Doyle's *The Adventures of Sherlock Holmes.*

"When I was your age," he said, feeling like an old man suddenly, "I used to get them all the time."

"The whole thing? Having to breathe into a paper bag and all?"

"The whole nine yards. I used to call hospital emergency rooms, convinced I was having a heart attack and they would tell me to go breathe into a bag and call them back in ten minutes if it didn't stop."

"I can't control my anxiety attacks," Leanna said. "And I don't know what starts them. Sometimes I'll just be sitting there in a restaurant and there will be a spot on a fork or something and then all of a sudden I feel my breath is, like, trapped in my chest and then it starts. It really freaks out my boyfriend because he's never been with anyone who has anxiety attacks."

"Uh, huh." Trace shook a smoke loose from the pack at the side of the chair and lit it.

"I had one on-set the other day and that was really embarrassing."

"Why? What happened?"

"I was doing this bondage thing and they had me tied up and they had these electric clamps attached to my nipples – "

"You do bondage movies?"

"Just this one." She flipped a stray strand of wet blonde hair off her forehead. "My agent got it for me but I told him never again. They told me they were going to shock my nipples and I didn't have a problem with that but then they turned up to a Six instead of a Four and I fucking freaked out."

"If I was a performer," Trace said for lack of anything else to say, "I would draw the line at movies like that."

"Like I said, it was a one-time thing only and I told my agent I don't want to do any more of those scenes."

Throughout the afternoon, Leanna's friends would stop by her chair and coo words of concern about her injury and offer tips on how to properly care for her wound once she got home.

"This is nothing," she repeatedly said. "I have a three-year-old at home so trust me, I know how to treat injuries."

But toward the end of the day, once her Vicodin kicked in, there came further embellishment to the story about the three-year-old at home in dire need of emergency treatment.

"Make sure you treat that with hydrogen peroxide and a good topical antibiotic," one of the cameramen lectured Leanna.

"This is nothing. I have a three-year-old at home. You know how many times we've had to take him to the emergency room? Jeez. He always comes tearing through the living room and hitting his head on the edge of the glass coffee table. It's happened three times now."

Leanna then turned to Betty, the girl who earlier had admired the way Trace's hand perfectly fit the handle of his cane.

"You just gonna hang out at home after this?"

"Yeah."

"Can I come with you? Maybe we can smoke a blunt or two? I'm feeling like shit."

"Sure, honey."

Trace picked up the book he was reading and pretended to have not heard the conversation. He took cold comfort in remembering that he had a bottle of Vicodin and at least three fingers of Kentucky bourbon awaiting him at home.

Toyland

"Trace, I just don't have sympathy for anyone complaining that they don't like their job. A lot of people don't like their jobs."

"You've been unemployed for too long."

"No shit."

"Look, Norman, I know a lot of people don't like their goddamn jobs but they still manage to get out of bed in the morning and at least fake it. It's a little different when – "

"Ah, the plight of the overtaxed creative mind."

"Sarcasm doesn't fit you well."

"I'm sorry, Trace. Are you going to order another drink?"

"Yeah. Can you do me a favor this afternoon?"

"Mm, hm. What d'you need?"

"My hands are all fucked up from psoriasis today. Can you swing by the hotel and make my bed and maybe wash some dishes? I'll give you twenty bucks."

"You don't have to pay me. But why don't you just take the Do Not Disturb sign off the door and let the maids in?"

"That's what I've been getting at. I can't do that. I'm not done writing the infomercial for New Vibrations. My room is still full of sex toys. About seventy pieces once I got them unpacked. Vibrators, dildos, lotions, gels – you name it. It looks like a goddamn sex shop blew up in there and there's simply no room to store it all. The shit is just laying out in the open until I figure out what to do with it."

"Isn't this considered a job perk?"

"If I was a chick, yeah."

"So, what's the problem with writing the piece?"

"Same thing. The premise is teaching potential or existing clerks in retail stores everything they need to know to successfully sell adult toys to customers."

"You ever work in an adult store?"

"Of course not. So I talked with Hal, the marketing director, on the phone this morning – and I have pages and pages of notes and a pretty good outline. All I have to do really is script it."

"Doesn't sound that difficult."

"It shouldn't be. But it will be."

"Why?"

"Because I burned out writing this shit years ago. That's why I don't do it anymore."

"But you're doing it again."

"I need the money."

"You're taking a wrong turn again, Trace."

"No shit. Can you do me one more favor?"

"What?"

"I need to swing by the Ninety-Nine Cents Store."

"What for?"

"Batteries. They didn't send any goddamn batteries."

Over a Shot of Rum

"You're like a boat at sea," Lisa said quietly. "There's no wind and you don't know which port you're going to drift to."

"That's about an accurate assessment," Trace replied, "except I know which port I'm gravitating toward."

"And it's not mine anymore."

He sighed. "Come on, that's not fair."

"I just want to know what's different."

"What's different how?"

"What's different about her that you've obviously responded so strongly to?"

"That's not fair. I'm not going to set you up for comparison with her and vice versa. It's all private anyway."

"It's all private?"

"Yeah, whatever is going on is private."

"Whatever is going on?" she mocked. "What does that mean?"

"I'm really too tired for this. Look, I like being friends and hanging out with you, okay?"

"Being friends and hanging out with me?" She had a habit of repeating his language back at him with a strong incredulous tone. "There was something between us at one time. What happened? What did I do wrong that she – "

"No. Don't go there. I'm not going to give you something to villainize me or to make you feel bad about yourself. I won't do it."

"So what you're saying is that all of your energy goes toward her from now on and I get none of it?"

"Didn't I just say I like hanging out with you, drinks at Acapulco and all that shit? We can still be friends, for chrissake."

Lisa looked at the floor and shook her head in the negative. "I have the answer I was looking for."

Alan Ladd and the Coyote Solitario Cantina

She was a floater.

The woman's body had sunk to the bottom of the old-fashioned claw-foot bathtub, remaining there under nineteen inches of water until it became bloated with gas and buoyant, floating back to the surface days later.

It had been an unusually warm November in L.A., so Trace figured it didn't take long for gas to form and rigor mortis to set in. The nails had already loosened from the fingers and toes. Her pupils were huge, dark, dilated orbs, gazing blankly at the stucco ceiling. The blue lips were slightly parted, as if in apology or prayer. She was completely naked, which always made the police suspect foul play, the theory being, until proven otherwise by autopsy, that bathtub suicides are normally clothed and nude bathtub suicides are the mark of a murderer trying to fake an accident. Drowning, Trace knew, is always a diagnosis of exclusion.

Trace noted a half-empty bottle of Old Grand Dad on the tiled bathroom floor. She had been drinking from a Dixie paper cup, washing down Seconal with the cheap bourbon. The Seconal bottle, located on the bathroom sink next to a biography of Alan Ladd, had recently been refilled at the Rite Aid pharmacy on West Sunset Boulevard. Trace picked up the Ladd biography in his gloved hands and studied the spine: Property of the West Hollywood Library. The checkout card was still intact inside the book. Like all of the other books in Mildred Spruce's lonely apartment above a long-closed Mexican restaurant on La Brea Avenue, the Ladd biography had been pilfered from a library in the L.A. County system.

The apartment was hot and the stench of decay was clinging to everything. Trace left Mildred floating in her watery grave and moved to the bedroom again. The drapes were thick and brown. When he pulled them aside he was sprayed with a fine mist of dust. The window was one of those old-fashioned frames with handles on either side that you pull upwards to slide the window up and open. Fresh air blasted into the room like it had been hovering outside for days, maybe weeks, desperate to gain entry. The sound of light Sunday traffic on the boulevard below filtered into the room. Everything was brown: brown threadbare carpeting, brown sheets and comforter on the overstuffed mattress, brown wallpaper with flecks of gold.

On the bedroom dresser was a crazy, crowded collection of framed photographs of the late film star Alan Ladd, many of them personally signed, always to someone other than Mildred Spruce.

"To Cynthia, All My Best, Alan Ladd."

"For Janine, Keep Your Chin Up! Best, Laddie."

"To Doris, my number one fan, Alan Ladd."

She probably bought them on eBay, Trace thought, or hounded them down through collectors' networks.

Weeks earlier, Trace had begun writing an essay for a film magazine comparing Ladd's titular character in the 1953 film *Shane* with Philip Seymour Hoffman's characterization of Truman Capote in *Capote*. There were, Trace told the magazine editor, distinct similarities. Shane is a mysterious stranger from parts unknown who comes into town and impresses the innocent and intimidates the hell out of everyone else. He doesn't dress like anybody they've ever seen before, doesn't speak in a manner they are accustomed to, and seems hell-bent on doing what he came there to accomplish.

But Trace got sidetracked in his research. He found himself immersed in the tragic life of Alan Ladd. *Shane* would represent the last quality motion picture Ladd would star in. The diminutive Hollywood leading man would commit suicide at his Palm Springs home on January 29, 1964, an overdose of alcohol and sedatives at the age of fifty.

"Every book about Alan Ladd is missing from the Los Angeles Public Library system," Trace told his editor one afternoon. "Not just biographies but any book that mentions Ladd or his movies. Gone. Vanished. Not checked out, but stolen."

"The entire system?" his editor asked, uncertain what this minor mystery had to do with a critical dissection of a mythical western film and a biopic of one of America's most gifted and strangest authors.

"West Hollywood, Hollywood, Mar Vista, and Culver City," Trace said.

Through the L.A. Public Library's online database, Trace cross-referenced the thefts. They began in Hollywood and moved steadily west. He tapped into the Santa Monica Library system. They had one copy, still on the shelves, of an obscure biography titled *Ladd: The Life, The Legend, The Legacy of Alan Ladd*.

"I'm staking out the Santa Monica library," Trace informed his editor.

"You're two weeks from deadline, Trace."

"This will be an interesting sidebar story. Don't worry. I'm not losing my focus."

For two days he patrolled the aisles of the Santa Monica main library, keeping a steady eye on that Ladd biography and taking sporadic breaks to eat stale hot dogs and drink sour black coffee from a vendor's cart in front of the building.

On the third day he saw her. He guessed she was about fifty, wearing a flowery housecoat and fluffy blue slippers. Her brown-blonde hair looked like a spider's nest, uncombed and unmanageable. She wore no make-up and she spoke to herself uncontrollably in barely-audible whispers, like a devout Jesuit at constant prayer, except her God was Golden Boy Alan Ladd and her holy writ was anything committed to paper on the man.

Trace leaned back on the opposing aisle next to a shelf of Erle Stanley Gardner's Perry Mason novels (Jesus Christ, that guy was prolific, Trace thought) and watched silently as Mildred Spruce simply dropped the Ladd biography into a large Trader Joe's canvas bag she was carrying.

He didn't alert security but followed Mildred Spruce to the exit, where she walked right around the security portal without any protest from the bored and lazy library staff. On Wilshire Boulevard she boarded a Big Blue Bus heading west.

Trace tailed the bus in his Packard. Mildred got off on La Brea near Hollywood and walked two blocks to the façade of Coyote Solitario Cantina, an old Mexican restaurant and bar that had been shuttered years ago. From the outside it reminded Trace of the haunted houses that various civic groups and rotary clubs used to put on at Halloween when he was a kid.

"Excuse me?" Trace called out to her at the mouth of the alley.

Mildred was hobbling down the alley toward the side entrance of the old restaurant. She turned at the sound of his voice and was startled by his presence.

"I'm not going to hurt you. I just want to know about the book."

She stared at him blankly. She didn't know what he was talking about; in fact, he could have been speaking in gibberish for all her understanding of human language in the grip of her madness, the insanity clear and definable on her prematurely aged face.

Trace tried another tactic. He pointed to the apartment window above the ghostly restaurant.

"Do you live here?"

She spun on her heels and scurried like a fat rat in a flowery housecoat toward the side entrance, fussing with a key that she kept on a string around her thick neck.

"Can I talk to you sometime?"

"Talk to me?" Her voice was harsh and phlegmatic.

"About Alan Ladd."

Her eyes then came alive. A smile appeared, revealing a row of uneven rotting teeth. She thought about his request for a moment, giving it long and due consideration.

"Tomorrow afternoon," she finally announced. "Two o'clock. We can have tea and watercress sandwiches and talk about Laddie. But now I have to go to bed. Goodbye."

Trace watched her retreat into the vermin-infested bowels of the building.

When Trace arrived the next day just before the appointed time he found the side entrance to the Coyote Solitario Cantina unlocked. He donned his black leather gloves by instinct. Or maybe the distinct smell of decomposition told him he would need to cover his tracks very carefully.

And there was Mildred Spruce, floating in the bathtub, every room in her small and musty apartment stuffed from wall to wall with Alan Ladd memorabilia and books about Alan Ladd and framed pictures and scrapbooks and old movie magazines. All about Laddie. Mad about the boy.

"It's a fucking museum," Trace muttered.

In the kitchen, an army of cockroaches swarmed over a Styrofoam container holding what was once a grilled cheese sandwich. A note, written in a shaky scrawl, had been secured to the container with Scotch tape.

"No library police are taking me to jail," the note read. "Goodbye, my dearest Laddie, and I hope and pray I will be seeing you soon. Yours in love ... Millie."

Trace sat down on a kitchen chair. It was an old metal frame chair with red vinyl padding and backing. He lit a cigarette and inhaled deeply as the hot November wind raced through the now-open kitchen window and threatened to dismiss the smell of death and decay.

"I really should mind my own business sometimes," he said to no one but himself and the slow parade of cockroaches.

Fear and Loathing in Studio City

They were somewhere near Studio City in the number two lane of the westbound 101 freeway when the drugs began to take hold.

"I'm not seeing this," Trace said in a low, modulated voice from the passenger seat. "Do you see that?"

Norman pumped a fist on the rim of the steering wheel, keeping time with a Tom Petty song booming over the car stereo.

> My name's Joe I'm the CEO
> yeah, I'm the man
> makes the big wheels roll
> I'm the hand on
> the green light switch
> you get to be famous
> I get to be rich

"See what?" Norman said.

"You don't see that guy doing handstands on his motorcycle?"

"Where?"

"Over there!" Trace pointed. "About a hundred yards up in that lane."

"I don't see it."

"What're you, blind?"

"In my left eye," Norman reminded Trace, "yes, I am."

"Are you stoned?"

"I never get stoned in the morning," the porn director lied.

Trace began his morning with a tab of Ativan, a strong anti-anxiety medication, and four quick tokes off the remains of a joint clumsily rolled the night before. He had resolved that the only way he could get through this momentary detour back into the Porn Ghetto was through an altered state of consciousness.

"I like that," Trace said. His head was tilted sideways and he was staring out the passenger window through glassy eyes.

"What?"

"I like the way the freeway retaining wall goes gliding by when you fix your eyes on it. It's like a panorama. A big brown and tan panorama."

Norman laughed. "You're stoned. Did you take that half an Ativan?"

"Half?" Trace blinked his eyes. "I took the whole thing."

"I told you to take half!" Norman scolded. "A full one'll put you to sleep."

"That's not a bad idea."

"Shit. I need you awake, Trace."

"Fine. Wake me when we get to the restaurant."

It had been a long time since Trace had eaten in Jerry's Famous Deli on Ventura Boulevard, a favorite Valley hangout for character actors, stand-up comics, sitcom writers, or basically anyone with a briefcase full of head shots or a résumé with box office charts attached.

"You honestly didn't see that guy doing handstands on his motorcycle?" Trace asked Norman as the waitress led them to a table at the back of the restaurant.

"Nope. You're stoned," Norman teased.

Trace noticed a famous movie star sitting in one of the plush red booths with an aging blonde woman who could have been a movie star at some point in her life, what with that stretched and sagging skin on her very familiar face that indicated one too many journeys under the knife.

Nip tuck, he thought.

The famous movie star she was lunching with looked a hell of a lot older in real life than he did on screen. The shelf life is almost expired on that career, Trace thought.

They were seated at a table across from the glass door that led to the bowling alley on the north side of the restaurant.

"Cool!" Trace enthused. "A bowling alley. I completely forgot there was a bowling alley here. Don't sit there!"

"What the hell?"

"I want that seat. It looks out on the bowling alley, gimme something to look at."

Trace was to be an executioner of sorts that day. He was almost through writing and producing the training video for sex shop workers with Norman. The show was being underwritten by the mammoth adult toy manufacturer, New Vibrations. The company had insisted on using legitimate, mainstream actors for the infomercial so Trace and Norman farmed the work out to a legitimate casting director. More expensive than placing an Acting Gigs ad on Craigs List – by about three thousand dollars – but a casting director knows exactly what type of actor you're looking for, saving you the time of wading through demo reels and head shots. Today was the day that Trace had to select one male and one female host for the show from a final callback of four men and four women.

"I keep forgetting you're blind in that eye," Trace said as he dumped two packets of sugar in his coffee and began craving a pastrami sandwich. He stirred the sugar into the coffee and listened to the sound of bowling balls striking pins. He thought the noise resembled that of a wave of water made of wood striking a linoleum beach. That made him think of soft Japanese wood prints and he let his mind wander there until Hal Blume, marketing director for New Vibrations, arrived at the table ten minutes late for the scheduled one o'clock meeting.

"Why is it every time I see you guys you're eating?" Hal asked with a truly perplexed look on his ruddy face. Fifty-seven years old, Hal had recently lost a significant amount of weight due to the surgical removal of half of his stomach for cancer.

"Maybe that's because we always meet in restaurants, Hal," Trace said as he bit into his hot pastrami sandwich. The food was good. Everything was good. Except for the fact that he would soon have to lay the rejection slip on six struggling actors.

"As writers we deal with rejection all the time," he told a friend a few days later, "but actors, they go through it day in and day out. Rejection after rejection, they're not right for a part for one reason or another. It has to be maddening and yet they crave the attention that acting brings so it's really a pretty fucking demented yin-yang going on."

Trace presented Hal with the latest draft of the script and then launched himself up from the table with the aid of his cane.

"I'll be back," he announced.

In the time it would take Hal to read the new script, Trace reasoned, he could take a nice leisurely stroll through the bowling alley. He liked to hang out in bowling alleys when he was a kid. The smell of bowling shoes and talcum powder and draft beer and sticky sweet Coca-Cola brought memories washing over him. But for Trace childhood memories were not a place to linger for any extended period of time so he made a retreat from the bowling alley after only a few moments and returned to the deli.

Express

Trace always used the express window at his bank branch, which often meant a longer wait than the line reserved for all trans-actions. One particular afternoon he stood in line behind seven other patrons. It was a slow move forward. It seemed that everyone was cashing a check, which is less of an "express" transaction than a straight deposit, which was what Trace had in mind.

As time ticked slowly by he leaned on his cane to support his broken frame. In what felt like an hour – but was probably closer to ten minutes in reality – he made it to the teller's window with his check and deposit slip. She was a pretty, dark-eyed young Armenian woman named Therese.

"I'm so sorry about the long wait," she said. It was one of the most sincere apologies Trace had ever heard.

"Perfectly fine," Trace replied. "It's a Monday, always a busy banking day."

Therese shook her head ruefully. No, it was not perfectly fine. She nodded to his cane.

"You shouldn't have had to stand for so long," she insisted. "Next time, get a manager to take your transaction for you. I am so sorry."

Therese was indeed so sorry. Trace was amazed that someone could accept that much personal responsibility for a stranger's pain and discomfort. She began processing his transaction and stared at the computer screen quizzically.

"There's something wrong with this account," she said. "It doesn't match."

Trace took the check from her and studied his endorsement and account number on the back.

"Yep, that's my account number."

She processed it again and shook her head after a beat.

"No, this is someone else's account."

Trace pulled out his checkbook and compared the account number to that he had scribbled on the deposit slip and the back of the check.

"Damn," he said, "I was giving you my ex-wife's account number."

Again, Therese would accept no humility from Trace.

"It's not your fault."

By the time Trace's transaction was complete there was a longer line at the express window than when he first arrived.

"Feral Along the Fault Line"

Trace had been asked to contribute an original short story for the annual anthology of an online literary erotica site, Curved Lips.com.

"Can you make it a Dan Knight story?" the editor asked enthusiastically over the phone. She was calling from Georgia and had that sweet little Southern lilt to her voice that Trace found neither sexy, engaging, nor interesting. All of the editors for Curved Lips lived in far-flung areas of the continental United States; in fact, one of their fiction editors was a wild-bearded man named Ray who lived in a tarpaper shack with no electricity in the Rocky Mountains. Ray used a solar-powered laptop and hunted for his own food. Trace called him The Unabomber.

"A Dan Knight story would require too much set-up, too much backstory," Trace told the editor. Her name was Missy. She owned the domain name Curved Lips.com, oversaw all editorial content – sometimes nixing a story that the other editors had already approved – and self-published the annual fiction anthology Trace was being asked to write for.

"Well, here's the theme, sugar," she sang into the phone. "Social Darwinism."

"I've written about Jack London and Social Darwinism before."

"Think erotica, sweetie. Jack London isn't erotic ... is he?"

Within thirty minutes of ending the discussion with Missy he already had the title he wanted to use for the original work. He raced over to the keyboard and typed it onto the blank screen:

FERAL ALONG THE FAULT LINE

Trace decided to write a piece that was an homage to some of his favorite authors from the Seventies: Marc Norman, Joan Didion, and, most specifically, the terrific Rudy Wurlitzer novella *Quake*, a harrowing tale of the violent aftermath of a great quake that lays L.A. flat.

So he had his title and his inspiration. Now all he needed was a story.

He made a cup of coffee, broke the band on a fresh pack of cigarettes, and settled in at the desk, staring at the title on the monitor:

FERAL ALONG THE FAULT LINE

Earthquake. Darkness. Night. A gun. Sex. Social Darwinism. He wanted to hook them with the opening line, pull them in and repulse them at the same time. If you asked Trace for a slice of erotica, you would be foolish to expect candies and flowers. He pounded out the opening in thirty seconds:

"Yeah! No!" she screamed. "There!"

She was on her hands and knees, elbows digging into the paisley bedspread on the living room floor. Her breath rose and fell in shallow gasps. Her long brunette hair, usually lustrous and full of bounce, was wildly spun in all directions, bringing to Kevin's mind the image of a compass that had been broken, its points shattered into dozens of pieces.

Trace paused, sipped his coffee and took a drag off the Marlboro. What kind of a social structure do these people inhabit? he wondered. Clearly Tabitha is exerting some kind of power over this Kevin fellow. He typed:

As usual, Kevin was struggling to keep pace with her manic sexual energy but an artist always does his best to please his patron.

Tabitha had been supporting Kevin for the last seven months, paying his rent, utilities, groceries. She even bought him a whole new wardrobe at a chic Sunset Plaza boutique despite the fact that his job — when he was working — required only a modest wardrobe that consisted of paint-smeared sneakers, ragged jeans, and denim coveralls.

Kevin was a painter whose specialty was interior residential and commercial walls. He looked upon exterior paint jobs as the domain for lesser artists and an artist is precisely what he was. You wouldn't find his one-man business in the Yellow Pages under "Painters." He was listed under "Artists."

"Get up, baby! Get on your knees!" Tabitha hissed.

Kevin got to his knees without question. She stood over him and announced his next task.

Now, this is getting edgy, Trace thought. The coffee was getting cold but there was no time to reheat it in the microwave. He was on a roll. He continued to pound at the black keyboard:

So, this was the "new thing" she said she wanted to try when they spoke on the phone that morning, Kevin thought. She had already found dozens of ways to humiliate him sexually — each one rising her to new plateaus of nirvana — so what was one more foray into sexual deviancy going to cost him? Nothing. It would pay his bills for the next month until he found another client willing to believe that he was more than just a house painter. Even though he was the only one capable of seeing it,

Kevin firmly believed that he brought an artistic sensibility to his interior flourishes with a paint can and a brush. That's why he demanded a rate three times that of what the market would bear.

That's why, he thought, I'm on my knees for this sick, deviant bitch.

Tabitha was yelling at him again when he heard the dishes in the kitchen rattling. At first he thought it was a truck rumbling by outside. Kevin lived in a small Lockheed-era home in Burbank on a busy main thoroughfare two blocks away from Warner Brothers. Monstrous studio grip and electric trucks were always rolling by his front door.

Then there was the initial jolt, not a rolling motion like most earthquakes he had experienced, but a hard jab that he felt in every bone in his body. The jolt knocked Tabitha down. She fell on top of him in a heap, shrieking, hair flying everywhere.

The small single-frame house trembled. To Kevin, it felt like a giant pair of hands had seized both sides of the house and were trying to shake the contents loose. Outside, Kevin could hear all manner of loud crackling and hissing noises as power lines fell, plunging Burbank into darkness.

Trace looked at what he wrote. A giant pair of hands? What about "two giant hands"? He thought about it for a few moments more, decided that it was just a silly metaphor for a silly anthology and moved on dismissively:

He could feel the house shifting and there was a noise in his head like the shriek of a jet engine. Tabitha screamed when a hanging plant shook loose from the ceiling, the ceramic pot shattering on the hardwood floor a matter of inches away from her skull. Kevin quietly cursed Tabitha's near miss with a cranial fracture.

Kevin struggled to get to his feet but terra firma was suddenly nothing more than a myth. The floorboards were moving like the keys of a player piano. Cracks and fissures were appearing on all four walls, the stigmata of powerful earth tremors.

After two full minutes the shaking was still going strong and that was when Kevin realized that this was no Chatsworth earthquake, no Whittier Narrows shaker, not even equal to the Loma Prieta endured up in the Bay Area in 1989. This was a major motherfucking earthquake. This was, without a doubt, the much-anticipated Big One.

He heard a symphony of chaotic noise in the dark night as the rumbling persisted. Car alarms wailing in protest. Glass shattering. The groaning of buildings surrendering to the strain, collapsing in weary resignation to their fate. There was a strange popping sound and the snake-like hiss of broken water mains and broken gas lines. He heard a car slam into a house across the street. If anyone in the house screamed in reaction to the sudden intrusion he couldn't hear it. In fact, he heard no human noises whatsoever, just the creak and groan and shriek and collapse of human machinery and architecture and he found it odd that at such a calamitous moment in human history not a human voice was to be heard other than Tabitha's labored breathing next to him.

And then it stopped as abruptly as it started.

Trace extracted himself from the desk chair and limped to the microwave. He nuked the cold cup of coffee, emptied and washed the ashtray, lit another cigarette, and promptly returned to work. He did not pause to read what he had previously written. He just kept going, as if on autopilot.

"Jesus Christ!" Tabitha blurted. Her nudity was a strange incongruity to the destruction inside the house.

"Put some clothes on," Kevin said with a punishing frown.

He gingerly made his way into the kitchen, sidestepping books that had been ejected from cases and onto the floor, shattered pottery, broken glass from the windows. That popping sound he heard but couldn't identify must have been the windows exploding.

Kevin kept very little food or dishes in the kitchen so the damage was minimal, except for the broken window and the sink, which collapsed into itself and was sending a jet of water into the air. Kevin found the bottle of Ketel One in the cabinet undamaged. He unscrewed the cap and took a long pull.

This is it, he thought, this is the one we aren't going to pull back from and dust ourselves off and move on to wait for the next one.

Within hours, he surmised, perhaps minutes, when people realized the extent of the damage, social order was going to break down. Los Angeles was going to become a living and breathing mass of social Darwinism and what did he have to contribute and to keep himself safe?

He found his gun under an overturned nightstand in the bedroom. At least he had that but a lot of other people in the quake-ravaged city would be armed too. It would take a long time for the federal government to get relief aid in and until that time there would be widespread looting, perhaps even house-to-house.

What would he have to offer when the roving hordes came to his quake-scarred door? What would he have to barter with to keep himself safe and warm and fed?

He returned to the living room to find Tabitha still nude. She had parked herself in a corner of the room with her knees drawn up to her chest. Her slender arms were draped across her knees. Her eyes were catatonic.

Her, his mind returned in answer to the questions. You have her to barter with, this sex-mad bundle of perversion and paraphilia is your meal ticket.

He just might get through this after all.

And there would be a huge demand for interior painters when the reconstruction process began.

THE END, he typed. He e-mailed the story to all of the fiction editors at Curved Lips, including the Unabomber in his dark mountain cabin.

Two weeks passed and he heard nothing. Finally, into week three, Ray, the Unabomber, sent Trace a sheepish e-mail:

"Trace,

"Terribly sorry we cannot run this fabulous piece. Unfortunately, my colleagues did not share my enthusiasm for your story. Most felt it was either misogynistic or pure pornography (yeah, go figure, huh, Trace?).

"Anyway, sorry I couldn't help you, buddy. Try us again next year with something maybe a little more toned down?

"Best,

"Ray."

"It's Social Darwinism!" Trace screamed at the e-mail on the computer screen. "It's a misanthropic enterprise either way you look at it!"

Trace only stood to lose a hundred dollars on the rejection so it wasn't the money that mattered. He simply hated having his writing misunderstood.

It was two o'clock on a Tuesday afternoon. There was still plenty of daylight left. Trace made a fresh cup of coffee and thought about his next Dan Knight story.

How would his alter ego, Dan Knight, handle the rejection? Trace wondered. He smiled at the image of Dan Knight loading his revolver and pulling out a map of the United States, planning his homicidal itinerary. First stop: Georgia. Next stop: that remote cabin in the Rockies.

Trace and the Christmas Shoppers

It was a dry and crisp Saturday afternoon with fifteen days remaining on the calendar before Christmas. Trace never paid much attention to calendars except for their usefulness in plotting a magazine deadline. There was a time when he always had a calendar next to his desk – usually bought at a fifty percent discount after the holidays – but he found that the numbers staring him in the face every day filled him with dread and anxiety. The rent was due on the first of the month. The payday advance had to be rolled over on the fifteenth. The bank loan payment was due on the eighteenth. There were always doctors' appointments on certain dates and lunch appointments and cocktail get-togethers and birthdays to remember. So he stopped buying calendars altogether and lived a relatively disordered week-to-week existence, jotting down on a legal pad what had to be accomplished in any given week, always ordered by day, not date.

He decided to walk the ten blocks to the Glendale Galleria to buy a new bathrobe that December afternoon. That was the first mistake. The L.A. air was dry and he was suffering from a bronchial ailment brought on by the inhalation of the white flecks of dead skin that cascaded off his body every morning. When his psoriasis was ragingly acute – as it had been lately – he spent the first few hours of every day sitting at the desk, quietly surfing the Internet for research on whatever he was working on at the moment and using an array of blunt instruments to scrape the dead skin from his legs and upper torso. He found that the bottom edge of a hard plastic Bic lighter worked best for this purpose. He stopped using a wooden fork years earlier after he suffered nerve damage in both legs from employing such a cruel implement.

"You just need to stop scratching so much," a doctor once told Trace with a jovial smile and a handclasp to the shoulder.

"And maybe you need to stop breathing so much," Trace countered. "Telling a psoriasis patient not to scratch is like telling someone with TB they need to stop coughing."

It wasn't until he was two blocks away from the mammoth indoor shopping mall that Trace realized how close it was to Christmas. On the narrow residential streets adjoining the Galleria the vehicle traffic was heavier than usual, cars swarming like slow-moving sharks in the vain search for a parking spot. Trace soldiered on regardless. He needed that new bathrobe, something bulky and warm to wrap around his scarlet and scaly white skin in the cold and dry winter evenings and mornings.

Inside the mall it was far worse than he imagined. There they were, the happy hordes of the healthy. Fat ones, skinny ones, families walking five and six abreast, unsupervised children, men and women shopping alone and happy couples shopping together. The task was going to be as difficult as trying to navigate through Disneyland in the summer.

Trace looked upon it as a game of hopscotch, navigating from one open space to another as he made his way toward the Mervyn's flagship at the eastern edge of the mall. He seized a piece of open space surrounding a woman pushing a baby stroller and used that gain in ground to shoulder past a Hispanic family strolling so slowly that Trace wondered if they thought they were in a park. Passing the slow strollers, he veered to the left where there was an open space near a jewelers shop.

"I need to buy a new cross," he heard a woman say as she grabbed her boyfriend or husband by the hand and pulled him into the jewelers.

Strange way to put it, Trace thought. Most people would say "crucifix."

He darted through another open space and made his way to the escalator to the second floor that led to the men's department at Mervyn's. The restaurants were also on the second floor. Fast food. Burgers, Chinese, pizza by the slice, stir-fry. There were long lines outside every food venue so he gave up on the idea of procuring anything to eat from the mall even if it was nearly three o'clock and he hadn't eaten all day.

Once inside the department store he grabbed the first bulky bathrobe he found and seized a place in line. The three cashiers were frenzied. The shoppers were impatient. When it was Trace's turn to step forward he made the mistake of hesitating for a beat, causing a woman standing behind him to snap "Next in line!" He glared at the woman and wished he had his cane with him. He was capable of causing a lot of mischief with his cane, little upsets and injuries that had the appearance of being accidental.

He fled the mall at the Brand Boulevard exit and began the ten-block walk home. Three blocks into his retreat he realized too late that he was walking at a pace too fast for his ailments, still employing the aggressive land-grabbing technique that had carried him through the hordes of Christmas shoppers. The dry December air was swooping into his bronchial passages afflicted with dead skin. He slowed his stride but already he felt his throat tightening. He tried to clear his throat but that only brought on a dry, hacking cough.

Trace always prided himself on being able to carefully disguise and conceal his ailment from the public but this wasn't going to be one of those days. He desperately needed water to clear the dry air in his throat but there was none to be found. He grabbed the edge of a bus bench with one gloved hand and began coughing with violent fury, looking every bit like the character he never wanted to be, a desperately ill man who needed bed rest instead of shopping with the hordes of the healthy and rushing to meet another magazine deadline and yet another and another after that, and promoting his book when not on a magazine deadline. Except for the two hours every night when Trace lathered his burning legs and torso with a Vaseline-like topical substance while watching a movie, his life was one endless deadline, one story after another to write, like some demented tribal elder chattering around the campfire, never knowing when to shut up but his ability with words was keeping everyone enthralled and it was paying his way through life so there it was.

Trace tried not to notice the reaction he was drawing from pedestrians and motorists, hunched over the bus bench as he expelled in loud barks and hacks the irritant in the back of his throat.

The coughing spell passed in less than five minutes. The slam to Trace's dignity would take much longer to go away.

It Doesn't Burn in Laurel Canyon

"Is there more?" Amy asked. More to the story, she meant, more to the story about that night.

"Of course there's more," Trace replied. "There's always more."

They emerged from the theater on South Dohney in Beverly Hills and he lit a cigarette. The first cigarette in over ninety minutes, not that Trace was counting the passage of time except where being in Amy's company was concerned. Ninety minutes. It would all be over in less than a half hour, a quick jaunt up Sunset and then over Laurel Canyon and then she would deposit him at his front door. Perhaps another week would pass before they could see each other again, before she would allow it, before her busy life would allow it.

In the parking garage Amy quickened her stride and walked several paces ahead of him.

"You can – " She began to say something and pivoted her head to see that Trace was stamping out the remains of his half-smoked cigarette on the cold concrete floor of the garage. "I was going to say you can smoke in the car if you roll the window down."

"Oh. Too late," he said with a soft smile.

They took Laurel Canyon across to the Valley, her squat black car gripping the road like a panther and she was in the driver's seat, both hands on the wheel, eyes on the asphalt as if searching for meaning in the white lines that her headlights picked up but really, actually, she was just concentrating on the serpentine twists and turns in the canyon night.

The radio was off. It was on during the entire drive to Beverly Hills, first a classical station and then a classic rock station that was playing a Led Zeppelin album. But now no music emanated from the dashboard sound system, just the noise of their own breathing and the night whooshing by outside and Trace wondered for a moment why the radio was off.

There was a catch in her voice when Amy said, "I always loved it up here. Here and Topanga Canyon, too."

"Topanga Canyon burns a lot," Trace said. "It doesn't burn that often in Laurel Canyon."

He didn't know if the last thing he said was empirically true but it sounded true. He honestly couldn't recall the last time he heard about a major fire in Laurel Canyon.

The houses were tucked on the side of the canyon wall like somebody's afterthought. Nice homes occupied by musicians, artists, writers, movie people.

Trace sighed.

"It would be nice to live up here," he said. "We just need to work on selling more books."

Trace rolled down the window and lit a cigarette, not because he wanted it but because he could.

Trace and the One-Armed Dancer

"No, sweetie, you don't understand." She leaned into the red jar candle on the table to light her Benson and Hedges. "I've never had a prosthetic arm. Never."

"Do they allow smoking in here?" Trace said.

"From what I know, they don't allow smoking indoors any-where in California."

"Aren't you going to get in trouble?"

"Honey, I'm the star attraction. I don't get in trouble. Smoke 'em if you got 'em, nobody's gonna say anything."

There were no windows in the small bar on Lankershim Boulevard and the owner didn't believe in a brightly-lit room. Dim spotlights suspended from the ceiling shone on the stage to the left of the bar where a bikini-clad dancer was shaking her cellulite-infested hips to a Rick James tune on the old jukebox.

"Why is it so dark in here?" Trace asked as he lit a cigarette.

"Skokie likes to keep the lights down low, says it hides the girls' what he calls 'imperfections'."

"Skokie" was Skokie Bismark, a man Trace knew and had little respect for. Skokie spent five years as a suitcase pimp, the name given to any husband, boyfriend, second cousin, putative father or other interloper of the male persuasion who leeches onto a porn star's career, crowns himself her manager, and then generally runs her career into the ground with all the reckless glee of a suicide bomber.

When Stella and Skokie divorced after six years of ill-advised marriage, Skokie surrendered all of the Stella Bismark websites to her in exchange for full ownership of the bikini bar they bought with her money. The rumor was that Skokie was bisexual and used the bar as a front to meet and date his prospective male lovers. At that very moment, Trace noticed, Skokie was sitting at a table in a far corner near the scratched and scarred pool tables with an awfully feminine-looking young man so perhaps there was some truth to the rumors after all.

"Speaking of imperfections – " Trace said and sipped his beer.

"It was a farming accident when I was a kid," she explained.

"You've got to be kidding me." Trace scribbled notes on a yellow legal pad.

The one-armed dancer laughed. Trace liked her smile. It lifted her stooped shoulders and made her eyes dance. He could see that once she must have been very attractive but now gravity was playing havoc with her natural D-cup and her long legs were a road map of varicose veins. Her face bore all the unkind ravages of substance abuse. He had it on good authority that she could suck a golf ball out of a garden hose but he also knew that she had been living in the same crappy and run-down apartment in North Hollywood for fifteen years, that her twenty-year-old son was a meth addict living on the streets of Hollywood, and that she was suffering from Hepatitis-C, so either her fellatio skills never served her well or she had been giving it away all these years.

"Seriously," she said. "I grew up on a farm in Iowa. Your readers don't wanna know the details, honey. Let's just say it was nasty and my arm was lopped off right at the shoulder. Pretty much a clean cut."

She snuffed her cigarette out in a plastic ashtray and lit another.

"Do you find that your – " Trace groped to find the right word.

"My defect?" she offered.

"If that's what you want to call it."

"Is it a draw?"

"Yeah. I mean, are there guys that are into – "

"Honey, there are guys that are into everything and anything. If you're asking if I've had guys who asked to fuck my stump I'd have to say yes."

Trace smiled. "I don't want to know what your answer was."

"Let's just say they don't make the kind of underarm deodorant I need."

Trace heaved a sigh and closed his notebook. He needed to get out of there and into the light. He swallowed the last of his beer and stood.

"Did you get everything you need?" The look on her face was imploring.

"Yeah. Just make sure that you get those photos over to the magazine in the morning. Skokie has the address."

As Trace carried himself to the door she spoke to his back.

"Y'all come back now," she said. And then she laughed.

The Most Wonderful Time
of the Year

It was three days before Christmas and Trace felt a black depression coming on.

"Jesus Christ," he muttered. "There wasn't enough left of her to put in a shoebox."

"Providing it's a child's size shoebox," Wellbeck confirmed. The Public Information Officer for the L.A. County Coroner's Office offered Trace a cigar from a simple glass humidor on his desk.

Trace proffered an aromatic Don Diego cigar with his free hand. In the other hand he held the seven-page coroner's report reciting in both gruesome and routine detail the cause of death of seventeen-year-old Deborah Hollingsworth.

"When is this being released to the family?" Trace's voice was hollow, almost a half-whisper.

"This afternoon," Wellbeck replied. "And the press push-out is tomorrow afternoon. Please don't write anything about it until then, okay? I'm only showing you this in advance because you're a mutual friend of Liffey."

Trace and Jack Liffey were old friends. In the mid-1990s, Jack Liffey lost his aerospace job, and then his wife and daughter. The only thing he had left was an innate ability to track down missing children. He set himself up as a child-finder, providing aid, comfort, and his considerable detection skills to grieving families whose cases didn't merit the attention of the local police for one aggravating reason or another.

Deborah Hollingsworth went missing one week before Thanksgiving after agreeing to a blind date with a suitor she met through an online personals ad. She was last seen at Sardo's in Burbank, blocks away from her mother and father's home on West Verdugo Avenue. She seemed neither particularly bright – a C average student in high school – nor particularly lacking in talent, judging from the heartfelt handwritten journals of prose and poetry that Liffey discovered hidden beneath the floorboards in the young woman's bedroom closet.

"A cut above your average teen angst," Liffey told Trace.

When the Burbank police hit one dead end after another Liffey asked Trace to write a story about the girl's disappearance for a true crime website that Trace often contributed to. He was happy to comply with the request but he now had doubts that he should ever have become involved – not after seeing the coroner's final report. The body of Deborah Hollingsworth was discovered in an oil field near Compton. The details of her death were simply and purely unspeakable.

It's a side effect of the job, Trace reminded himself as he approached his Packard in the fenced-in parking lot of the Coroner's Office on San Fernando Road. Sometimes you are compelled to see things better left unseen.

He folded the coroner's report neatly, placed it in the glove compartment, lit the Don Diego cigar and drove. It didn't feel like Christmas in L.A. Johnny Mountain, the improbably named meteorologist for the local CBS-TV affiliate, promised a high of eighty degrees on Christmas Day. The air was as dry as the inside of a wino's bottle of Thunderbird.

Trace drove west on Alameda Avenue, passing the Walt Disney Studios. The compound was surrounded by a wrought-iron fence topped by ominous-looking wrought-iron spears twisted into the shape of Mickey Mouse's head. The locals called the studio Mouse-Schwitz. A few blocks ahead was St. Joseph's Medical Center, where Trace's estranged daughter was born twelve years before during a torrential January downpour that lasted for weeks and flooded surface streets and freeways. It was a complicated labor, Trace recalled, because his wife had insisted on an epidural the moment labor pains set in. Gina always had a low tolerance for pain, physically or emotionally, and she carried the psychic scars left by her first husband who had fatally ventilated his chest with a shotgun when she initiated divorce proceedings.

At Hollywood Way, Trace hung a right and drove north. Within minutes his tires were crunching gravel in the driveway of the simple single-family dwelling on West Verdugo.

"Do you remember me, Mr. Hollingsworth?"

The old man regarded Trace through vacant eyes hemmed in by wire-rim bifocals. There was no blood in his face. Some invisible force seemed to be holding the fifty-seven-year-old father erect because he didn't appear to have the strength to live anymore, let alone get out of a chair to answer the door. He was a constantly churning factory of grief.

"Of course." Mr. Hollingsworth extended a palsied hand to Trace. "You're the magazine writer."

"It's about the coroner's report, sir."

"Yes. Yes. We're supposed to see it to – "

"Please, this is important. Listen to me. You know your daughter was murdered, right? I mean, the police have obviously told you that much and it's been all over the news."

The old man was confused.

"That's all you need to know, Mr. Hollingsworth," Trace continued. "Honestly. Trust me. I've read the report, sir, and I don't think you need to know the details."

Water was appearing at the edges of the old man's eyes.

Trace exhaled with a force he never knew his tobacco-charred lungs to possess.

"Please, sir," Trace pleaded. "Don't read it."

Trace drove home in a haze like none he had ever experienced before. Stumbling into the hotel elevator and pushing the fifth-floor floor button, his senses were assaulted by Christmas Muzak. The radio station was broadcasting a cheery rendition of 'It's the Most Wonderful Time of the Year.'

The depression was deep and intense, a cruel hammer blow to the soul. The girl had been reduced to scatterings, not even enough to place in a shoebox. As long as it's a child's-size shoebox, Wellbeck had said.

Trace knew, as he smoked and restlessly paced the length of his hotel room, that it wasn't the cruelty of the act that sent him into the black clouds. People were proving themselves savages in new and unique ways every day.

He called Felicity, a friend from his days in porn. A former star of the so-called Golden Age of Porn, when X-rated movies were screened in theaters and the seats were filled with couples, not rain-coat-clad perverts, Felicity Xavier made a living these days as a spiritual consultant and yoga instructor.

"It's the reduction, Trace," she purred over the phone. "Reduced to a shoebox. Isn't that what you said? Don't let the blackness deter you. You're in an expansion cycle with your career and the old trusty standby monsters are pissed."

"Um ... explain, please? Standby monsters?"

"Monsters meaning voices in our heads. Voices are just as capricious as angels. They can whisper true things, or they can whisper untrue things, but they tend to recycle their material. Hence, 'standby'."

Trace poured a glass of wine and listened carefully.

When we experience emotional and physical abuse, Felicity explained, even after we get away from the people who were mean to us, we are not off the hook, because we unconsciously create psychological replacements for the real people who were saying things to us that hold us down.

The wine was tart. Trace bought it at the corner market for $7.99 even though he knew it was sold at the 99 Cents Store for much less.

"We do that," Felicity continued, "because sometimes vile things are said to us by people we care about, or are 'supposed to' care about. On a biological level we want to please the people we care about, so, if a real person isn't there to tell you your entire life's work is nothing that wouldn't fit into a shoebox when all is said and done, a voice inside your head is created to carry on the important work of keeping you down."

Trace paced the room, phone clutched to his ear. He paused to consider the tiny Christmas display he created on the bookshelf near the front door. A plaster cast of Santa Claus and a bunch of cheap cardboard Christmas toys.

"Felicity," he said with a sigh, "can we cut to the chase?"

Felicity paused a moment to prepare her summary.

"You said your depression kicked in when you read the autopsy report and had a conversation about the victim filling a shoebox. What I'm trying to say is, you have more than a shoebox filled and you are not dead yet."

ACT THREE:
January – December 2006

Trace Goes Shopping

The corner market that Trace frequented was called Flynn's. It was the ghost of an old-fashioned neighborhood market, complete with butcher's counter, frozen food aisles, and a giant beer refrigerator. But the owners of the last fifteen years – two Korean immigrants, husband and wife, who only spoke in English in grunts and rapid gestures – closed down everything but the beer cooler and used the butcher's counter to sell an odd collection of stuffed animals and costume jewelry and cheap toys that no child would ever want.

There was no heat in the winter at Flynn's Market and no air conditioning in the sweltering L.A. summer. In the summer the baked goods such as bread and packaged pastries turned to mold within two days of hitting the shelves. Trace once bought a can of Campbell's Soup at Flynn's Market and discovered upon returning home to the hotel that the contents had expired … two years prior.

But Flynn's market was the only game in town in that Glendale neighborhood bordering on Griffith Park, the only market within walking distance of the hotel and the elementary school across the street. So people put up with the stale bread and lukewarm beer and they bought the stupid sweatshop T-shirts (two for five dollars) that adorned the top of what was once the butcher's counter and they endured the crude cave man grunts of the Korean owners that had some very vague resemblance to hospitality and basic human-to-human contact.

After fifteen years, the Koreans decided to call it a day and sold Flynn's Market to a handful of Armenian small businessmen. It took them two months to gut that dive market and convert it into a full-fledged neighborhood market. The butcher's counter was beautifully restored, sparkling chromium, glass, and steel. There was a fresh fruit and produce section, stocked daily. The Armenian owners were friendly and pleasant and appreciative of their customers, which were plenty after the Grand Opening.

Under the new Armenian ownership, Flynn's Market was a success, a corner store for the Armenian-American citizens within walking distance – and with an estimate of nearly two hundred thousand Armenians living in Glendale, Trace figured that the new owners probably pulled in one hundred customers per day easily just from those living within blocks of the market.

Trace liked the new owner, a tall, lanky, mustached Armenian in his early fifties. The man went out of his way to let Trace know how much he appreciated his daily patronage.

One Saturday afternoon in an unusually warm January, Trace was engaged in any number of activities to avoid confronting his four looming magazine deadlines for the month. He surfed the net. He read a few chapters of a novel. He cleaned his desk and used a spray can of cleaning duster to eject the dead skin from his keyboard. He was in the exfoliation phase of his latest psoriasis flare-up, a phase when the patient's skin begins to flake in finite amounts and fall off like so many snowflakes. The flakes fell in little clouds from his legs, his lower torso and, of course, his hands.

In the process of cleaning his desk he came across a study on psoriasis in literature written by a general practitioner in The Netherlands. The paper had been submitted to the Dutch College of General Practitioners.

"Psoriasis functions as a metaphor for the creative process," Trace read. "Psoriasis is the result of the implosion of the artist and the literary works on psoriasis – John Updike's *The Centaur* and *From the Journal of a Leper*, Dennis Potter's *The Singing Detective* – all cultivate the idea that psoriasis is the Achilles heel of the introvert individualist, the artist who looks upon the world as a guardsman from the ivory tower of his psoriasis. His salvation is make-believe or an entirely private world: the imagined past of the world of art."

Trace had forgotten he had a copy of that study. It was sandwiched between a phone book and two other ignored manila folders. He placed it in the file stacker to the left of his desk, resolving to read it again that evening, but as four o'clock was looming it was time for him to head to Flynn's Market for his six-pack of beer, pack of smokes, juice for the morning, and whatever else caught his eye.

Going out was an ordeal, as usual, that involved protecting his hands with leather gloves so the afflicted skin didn't break open and bleed in some less than holy stigmata as he carried the plastic grocery bags back home. The gloves also served another purpose: to prevent fast food cashiers and store clerks from recoiling in horror at the red, scaly, inflamed mess that represented his hands. On several occasions the clerks or cashiers would refuse to meet his extended hand and they laid the money down flat on the counter. They didn't know that his fingers couldn't bend to scratch and scoop up the cash without hurting himself. They were literally adding injury to insult.

That Saturday at Flynn's he grabbed his beer and a few other spare items and approached the checkout.

"Good evening," the owner beamed from behind the counter. Always with a smile and nod and a look in the eye. There was a European lilt to the way he said it: Good eve-un-ing.

Trace exchanged greetings with the owner and handed his groceries to the clerk, a short, plump, middle-aged Armenian woman who only worked on weekends. She spoke halting English, a handicap she always tried to allay with a wide and welcome smile.

Trace leaned his gloved hands on the gray marble counter while she tallied his groceries. Even with the gloves on, bright red patches of psoriatic skin were visible on his arthritic wrists. Suddenly the clerk turned to the owner and let loose in Armenian. She was telling him something with barely-suppressed urgency. The owner listened to her and nodded his head thoughtfully and then addressed Trace:

"She wants to give you something," he explained. "Please wait a moment."

Trace cocked his head in curiosity as the woman rummaged through her battered Gucci purse and extracted a packaged tube of prescription medication.

"It's for your hands," the owner said.

The woman handed the package to Trace with an enthusiastic nod of her head. It was a brand new tube of Betamethasone ointment, a topical steroid ointment that he had never tried before, suitable for eczema and psoriasis. The language on the package was in English and a whole series of Middle Eastern languages that looked like hieroglyphics but it was the real deal and with medications already straining his budget he was glad for any help he could get – even if it came from such an unexpected source.

"Thank you," he said, grabbing the groceries in his gloved hands and marveling for just one moment at how people really can sometimes surprise you with their sudden gestures of humanity. It's even more startling, he thought, when it's someone you barely know.

But she's an exception to the rule, Trace told himself as he walked back to the hotel, a kind exception to the rule.

Trace and the Twelve Apostles

"I'm not really keen on Christianity," Trace professed in carefully measured words.

"And yet you can't deny the power of *The Passion of the Christ*."

"Sure I can. I never saw it and I don't intend to see it."

"So you're the one," the young screenwriter said with a soft smile. "I'll get a copy of it for you. We have several loaners up at the house."

"The House" was a small gated home in the Hollywood Hills that the screenwriter, Casey Burrows, purchased with the proceeds of his first spec screenplay sale, a one-and-a-half-million-dollar pre-emptive bid by one of the majors for *The Idiot Twins*. The script was a lowbrow comedy that was rumored to be the movie that would put Jim Carrey solidly back on the block. For that reason alone, Trace hated Burrows.

"You have to come up to the house for one of the meetings, Trace. You just might get something out of it, you know."

This is like a bad joke, Trace thought. What's worse than a room full of aspiring screenwriters? A room full of born-again Christian aspiring screenwriters who believe that the power of faith and prayer will elevate them from obscurity – where most of them probably deserved to remain – to pitch meetings with Mel Gibson.

"Look at it this way," Casey persisted, "we can use you as a motivational speaker. Your career is very inspiring to other writers."

"Me? You're the one who sold a script for a million-five."

"The power of prayer, Trace. But look at you. Heck, you're almost Biblical in nature. You renounced the stability of a settled life to pursue a higher inner calling. And you succeeded by sheer force of will. I think the guys would love to hear anything you have to say."

The guys that Casey referred to were younger than Trace imagined they would be. Many of them were still being courted by acne and they all had that dumbstruck, starry-eyed look that many creative types have when they still believe that the cream always rises to the top, that talent alone is all it takes to have their own home in the Hollywood Hills.

"This is Trace," Casey announced to the twelve young men lounging in his living room.

Casey and his twelve apostles, Trace thought.

"Hello, Trace!" They spoke as one. Trace felt like he was at an AA meeting.

Trace nodded curtly and studied the spines of the DVDs that stood in for books on the oak-paneled living room bookshelf. *Silence of the Lambs* was inserted between *The Ten Commandments* and *Ben-Hur*. And there was David Lynch's *Blue Velvet* resting next to *The Greatest Story Ever Told*. Trace wondered where Casey hid the porno.

"Do you need a Bible, Trace?"

"Huh?" He turned to face the assembled group once more and they were all clutching Bibles in their hands.

"We do a small prayer service before we start the meeting," Casey explained. "Would you like to join us?"

"A Bible? I've already read it, thanks though. The New Testament has a bummer of an ending but I won't give it away. I'll just go get some coffee."

Casey instructed the young scribes to turn to the Book of James, Chapter Five, Verse Fourteen, to offer a prayer for the sick. Trace hiked his shoulders, thrust his hands deep into his pockets, and ambled into the kitchen.

Casey's young wife, Donna, was tending to the Mr. Coffee in the dark brick-and-wood kitchen. Trace knew Donna when she was better known as porn star Raven DeLuxe. Trace introduced Casey to Raven on the set of a triple-X film he wrote. At the time, Casey was an eager production assistant who invoked the name Jesus Christ quite frequently but never in a holy context.

"How's tricks?" Trace asked with a grin.

"Be nice," Donna warned.

"Jesus. That's the thing about ex-porn stars. So sensitive."

She was wearing a strapless dress that exposed the Horny Little Devil tattoo on her left shoulder.

"Shouldn't you cover that up?" Trace said.

"They've all seen it before. We all make mistakes, Trace. The difference is that some of us are forgiven."

"I see."

When Trace returned to the living room he found that the group of doe-eyed wanna-be scribes had been silently awaiting his return.

"Prayer time over?" Trace said. He sipped his coffee. It was bitter, even with milk and sugar added. Starbucks blend, he thought, every damn coffee maker these days is trying their hand at replicating the Starbucks House Blend.

"You want my thoughts about the writing life, correct? That's why I'm here?"

Casey nodded. The twelve remained silent, their eyes riveted on Trace.

"Okay. I'm forty-seven years old. I live in a nice residential hotel in a room about the size of your average studio apartment. When I don't eat out I cook my meals in a microwave. I wash my dishes in the bathtub – that is, when my stress-induced psoriasis allows my hands to touch water."

His stomach protested when he took another sip of the bitter coffee.

"This year I reached a milestone. I went from having bad credit due to IRS liens to having no credit whatsoever. None. All the bad debts fell off and I'm not sure which is worse, having bad credit or no credit at all."

They were hanging on to his every word.

"I have a twelve-year-old kid I never see, though we do trade e-mails every now and then. My own father – my birth father – was an absentee parent so I guess I'm just following what I learned growing up. I've been a drinker most of my life but these days it's just beer and wine – always remember that top shelf wine is better for you than anything that comes in a jug, write that down – and I pace my drinking in the evening with a little herbal remedy, if you know what I mean."

He finished the coffee and placed the empty cup on the bookshelf next to a stack of screeners of *The Passion of the Christ*.

"About forty percent of my monthly income goes to health maintenance – prescription meds for high blood pressure, the psoriasis, which I already mentioned, and a small host of other assorted maladies. I used to have good medical coverage through the Writer's Guild but I became an inactive member – meaning no one reputable has hired me to write a screenplay in years – so I lost my benefits."

Their faces were becoming slack.

"But here's my advice to you: Write. If you want to be a writer, just write. Every day. Write. Accept no other work until the person comes along that recognizes you as a writer, hires you as a writer, and you're on the road."

He slipped the black leather gloves out of his coat pocket and pulled them onto his hands, peeling away layers of dead skin in the process. He watched as the skin flaked off and drifted down onto the Oriental carpet at his feet.

"I have to go," he said quickly and quietly. "I have a meeting early in the morning and a looming deadline."

"We'll pray for you, Trace," Casey called out as Trace started for the door.

"You do that." He turned to face the room one last time. "And good luck to all of you. You're going to need it."

Baby Maria

Trace popped a Doxepin and slowly began to dress. He opted for jeans and an NYPD T-shirt but he had to throw a jacket over the short-sleeved shirt because of the bright red psoriatic lesions on his wrists and forearms.

"No need to scare the citizens," he muttered as he pulled on a pair of black sneakers with a great and painful effort. Tying the shoes was the hardest part – gripping those laces in his cracked and bleeding fingers – and he vowed to buy shoes with Velcro laces next time.

He completed the ensemble – baseball cap, black leather gloves, walking stick – and started out the door for the two-mile walk to the pharmacy on Brand Boulevard. He had a fresh refill of pain meds to pick up.

Trace had to rely on the cane frequently on the walk back to the residential hotel as his left ankle was swelling from the effects of psoriatic arthritis. Passing through the lobby, he saw a lone tenant waiting for the main elevator. Trace knew her. She was an Extended Stays regular and a certified loon. He had no desire to be trapped in an elevator with the old woman for five floors; in fact, he was in a downright antisocial mood and desired nothing more than to be back in his room with his swollen foot elevated.

He headed for the elevators on the southwest side of the hotel, the freight cars usually frequented by the housekeeping and maintenance staff. Trace kept himself on good terms with most of the hotel staff. A few of the housekeepers – all of them Hispanic with limited English skills – were disgusted by the bloody sheets and mounds of shed skin to be found in his bed every day but they still treated him with respect and he always tried to return the favor. It was most important for Trace to stay in the good graces of the front desk staff, the young men and women who controlled the mail, package and messenger deliveries, maintenance requests, and overall security.

At the southwest elevator Trace found Raphael waiting with an empty luggage cart. A short, bearded, and muscular Mexican-American who spoke English in heavily accented halting gasps, Raphael had been working at the hotel for as long as Trace could remember. "Raffi," as Trace called him, was the overworked concierge, which in Extended Stays Speak meant he was the bellhop, airport shuttle driver, messenger, and room service waiter.

"Hello, Raffi," Trace greeted through a painful grimace. He knew that now was the time to ask. Raffi would know. Raffi would be able to tell him what the story was behind that picture at the front desk. Every day for the last week, whenever Trace went to the lobby to pick up his mail, there was a framed photo of a beautiful baby girl, dark eyes shining, a smile as wide as can be. Next to the framed photograph was a small shoebox done up in Easter colors – pink and green and pale blue – with a small slot cut into the top of the box. In neat calligraphy on the front of the box someone wrote:

IN MEMORY OF BABY MARIA

ALL DONATIONS GRATEFULLY ACCEPTED

Someone – one of the front desk staff clearly – had lost a child. A baby. Trace knew it would tear him apart no matter who it was but he was too frightened to ask any of the desk staff for fear that he might accidentally ask the recipient of such awesome grief.

"What's the story with the baby, Raffi?"

"You know Graciela?" Raffi said.

Trace indeed knew Graciela. She was a kind and round-faced Mexican-American in her twenties. She was shy and soft-spoken and had been a great help to Trace on numerous occasions. She and her husband, Raffi explained, had enjoyed Christmas vacation in Mexico with their two-year-old daughter, their only child. There was an accident on the drive back to Los Angeles. Graciela escaped with a few broken bones and her husband also survived.

"But the baby, she died," Raffi said. "In the hospital, they gave Graciela the baby in a small box."

"Jesus Christ," Trace hissed and slumped against the wall just as the elevator doors slid open.

Back in his room, Trace rested for a few hours. He had no looming deadlines and nothing on his calendar that week except for another get-together with some colleagues at the Tam O'Shanter and a meeting with a movie executive. When it looked like the swelling in his foot had gone down enough for him to make his nightly trek to the corner market for beer and a pack of smokes he pulled on his jacket and paused to scrawl a note on the back of one of his business cards.

"I grieve for you and your husband," Trace wrote carefully. The pen was painful to grip in his swollen fingers and he hoped the words would come out legible. "I know it's not much but please fill in your name on the enclosed check and accept with my great sadness for your loss."

Trace wrote a check for twenty-five dollars, folded it neatly, and used a paper clip to attach the card to the check.

The framed photograph of the happy baby girl greeted him at the desk once more. Now there was a name attached, a brief life attached, a goddamn tragedy attached. He slipped the check and business card out of his jacket pocket and tried to slide the clipped items into the slot in the top of the donation box but the opening was too small. He removed his gloves, exposing his gnarled and blotched hands to the young clerk in front of him, and tried once again.

"I can't seem to get this into the box," Trace complained. "Do you have an envelope?"

The girl presented Trace with an envelope and he unceremoniously deposited the check and card and handed it to her.

"Would you just make sure that Graciela gets this, please?"

"Did you put your name on it so she knows who it's from?"

"Does it really matter?" Trace said. He leaned on his cane and started for the exit.

No Problem

REVEAL THE NARRATOR the editor had scribbled across the top of the page with a bright red felt tip marker.

Trace tossed the returned manuscript on the desk and reheated his third cup of morning coffee in the microwave. The coffee tasted bitter but everything left a bitter taste in his mouth when he was sleep-deprived.

Trace had Bradley Bozeman's office number programmed into the speed dial function on his cell phone, a good thing that day considering that his tired, hooded eyes were incapable of making out the small numerical digits on the keypad. Bozeman was the fiction editor for *Bay Point* magazine, a privately funded monthly literary supplement for a small town newspaper in Northern California.

"I don't want to reveal the narrator," Trace growled into the phone in lieu of a greeting when Bradley answered.

"You have to, Trace," Bradley countered. "It's Composition 101."

"Bullshit. Where did you go to school?"

"San Diego State. You?

"I didn't finish school," Trace muttered, opening an invitation for the editor to deride Trace's lack of education or perhaps open a discussion on the limitations of autodidacts. It was an invitation that Bradley declined, much to Trace's weary relief.

"Just think about it for a day or two, okay? Please. The narrative voice is unreliable if we don't know who it is."

"For Christ's sake, Bradley, I'm the narrator. The Dan Knight stories are about me."

"All the more reason they should be written in first-person narrative."

"What? And turn the Dan Knight stories into Dear Diary episodes? I don't think so."

"How's the weather down there?"

"Cold and cloudy," Trace complained.

"Same up here. You coming to San Francisco any time soon?"

"I don't know."

"Everything else cool with you?"

"Other than the fact that I can't seem to sleep past 5:00 A.M. lately," Trace said. "Yeah, everything's good."

"Insomnia?"

"I don't know what the fuck it is."

After a few more minutes of inane banter and another request from Bradley for Trace to "reveal the narrator," Trace hung up the phone and sat down at the desk. His limbs felt heavy and cumbersome. His eyelids fluttered and closed, demanding sleep, but a sudden and sharp arthritic stab in his left leg made sure he was wide awake once more.

Trace pushed some papers around on his desk to create the impression that he was getting something accomplished. He sipped his lukewarm coffee, lit a cigarette, and stared out the window at the L.A. skyline.

He missed Amy. She was on location in Huntsville, Alabama, ensconced in a cheap motel room, furiously pounding out a rewrite on the screenplay adaptation of her own novel for a rag tag band of independent film makers. She didn't know how long she would be gone, Amy had told Trace when he drove her to LAX two weeks prior, and she preferred that they keep e-mail correspondence and telephone calls to a minimum during her absence.

"Don't you think we could use a small break from each other?" she had asked.

"That could be a problem," Trace said. "I see you so little as it is."

She contorted her frame in the passenger seat so she was facing Trace. "It's your use of the word 'problem' that I think is the problem here. Seriously, you don't think it's a good idea?"

"Yes, it might be a good idea," Trace had relented. "But what did you mean by the whole 'problem' thing?"

He could tell that he was beginning to frustrate her.

"I meant, Trace, that you said it was a problem about not wanting to take a break and if you're saying that then it must be. So, yes, a break is a good idea."

Trace gripped the Packard's steering wheel hard. "Look, I misspoke, okay? There's no problem."

"Uh, huh."

"There isn't. There is no problem, Wags."

She smiled. "I know there is no problem. Honestly. I do. But I'm getting addicted to you. I think I need the break."

Trace remained silent for the next mile and a half as he processed her "addicted to you" comment.

"I can't sleep past 5:00 A.M. lately," he finally said. "No matter what time I go to bed, I wake up at five o'clock in the morning."

"That could be a problem."

Trace laughed. "Let's not get started on that word again."

Two weeks had passed now and an exhausted Trace decided to lift the embargo on communication with Amy. She sounded as tired as he was when she answered the motel phone in Huntsville.

"Bozeman wants to buy one of the Dan Knight stories but he wants me to make the narrative voice more clear."

"How much more clear? There's nothing wrong with the narrative."

"He thinks they should be written in first person."

There was a pause on the other end of the line. Trace could hear the rustling of paper. Amy was probably rifling through the script she was rewriting.

"First person?" she repeated.

"Yeah."

"Well," she sighed. "That could be a problem."

Blind Gunman

"What did the blind gunman do before he became a blind gunman?" the producer asked.

"Well, it's not like a blind gunman is an occupation in and of itself," Trace said with a thin smile.

"Of course not. Who'd want to hire a blind gunman?"

"But if it was this blind gunman you'd want to hire him because he's the best."

It was too early into the pitch meeting to gauge how well things were going but at least Trace had sold him on the blind assassin pitch. The producer was at least ten years younger than Trace and he wore his arrogance like an overcoat that was two sizes too large and ten years out of style. Not one of the four films he had produced to date had recouped their initial investment. His college degree was in business management, a field that rarely produces literary minds, but the entertainment industry is a business when all is said and done. In a meeting like this, Trace believed, it was really a matter of convincing an auto manufacturer that the nuts and bolts in a writer's mind will create next year's best-selling model.

"His blindness is an asset, not a handicap." Trace explained. "He compensates for his lack of sight with other heightened senses."

"Maybe he was a blind jazz musician before he became a blind gunman," the producer enthused.

Outside of the movies Trace had never seen a blind jazz musician and although he knew they must exist he felt we were already veering precariously into the valley of cinematic clichés.

But who cares what I think? Trace considered. The producer had already grabbed the ball and was running far afield with it.

"We could set the movie in post-Katrina New Orleans." There was a hint of excitement in his voice. "Lots of jazz history there."

"And Gothic architecture and voodoo and Mardi Gras."

"Maybe do some sort of a hallucinatory graveyard scene like in *Easy Rider.*"

A movie producer with a familiarity of films made before 1990. A rare bird indeed, Trace mused.

"What if his blindness was caused by a horrific explosion during a firefight and it left him with crippling pain, really horrific pain, that he sometimes uses drugs to combat?" Trace was in freefall. "And while he's on the drugs – think something hallucinatory like peyote – he has visions that give him an edge over his opponents."

"So," the producer leaned forward in his chair, another hint that he was getting more deeply involved in the story, "you're saying he was a sighted gunman before he was a blind gunman?"

"Sure."

"This is getting kinda superhero-ish. Like *Daredevil.*"

"Yeah, but I'm thinking more like Samuel Jackson instead of Ben Affleck."

"So he's black?"

"Why not?"

"A black blind jazz musician turned black blind gunman?"

"It works."

The producer rested his elbows on the desk, clasped both hands together and rested his chin upon them. "Smart. Do you know how many black people buy movie tickets every year?"

"Not off hand."

"Me either. But it's a lot. Now, if he's a hired gunman before he got blinded – is it got blinded or gets blinded? – how does the blind jazz musician thing fit in now?"

"That's his cover, a jazz musician, a guitarist that plays in a band down in the Latin Quarter."

Now Trace had him confused.

"If he's black, why does he play in the Latin Quarter?"

"Because that's where the jazz is ... or was?" Trace ventured. He could see a lot of research on New Orleans in his future.

"What if he's Latin then?"

"Orlando Bloom?"

"Too pretty. I don't see him as a blind gunman."

"Mark Anthony?"

"Who?"

"Musician and actor. *Bringing Out The Dead.*"

"Tanked at the box office."

And then they both said it at the same time:

"Antonio Banderas!"

A huge smile from the producer. A winning smile. This is going to be a done deal, Trace was thinking, steak tonight instead of Burger King. But then the producer shifted in his chair in a reasonable facsimile of severe discomfort.

"Wait a minute," the producer cautioned. "Banderas was in that *Once Upon A Time in Mexico*. Didn't Johnny Depp play a blind gunman in that?"

"Well, yeah, he gets blinded in the third act – I mean, way close to the climax, right? – but his character is not a blind gunman, *per se.*"

"But he is."

"He is what?"

"A blind gunman."

"Okay." Trace threw the next hook in the water. "What if he's a deaf gunman instead?"

Burned

"What I don't understand is how the fire jumped all the way over here."

Trace poked with his cane at the charred remains of a stack of rackjobber paperback books. The covers of the books were singed but intact, lurid gay porn titles with even more lurid charcoal renderings of homoerotic art.

"The fire didn't jump over here," Trace said. "This was a separate fire."

Greg chewed on his thick lower lip for a beat. He didn't like Trace's answer.

"What does that do to my theory?"

"Shoots it to shit, Greg, unless you think these books spontaneously combusted as well."

As actors go, Trace felt, Greg Harrington was a smart one. He always kept his ego in check and was painfully aware of his limitations as a thespian. When his big break finally arrived – a lead role in an ill-fated sitcom – Greg saved every dollar he could and bought a piece of income property in North Hollywood, a duplex with an apartment over the garage in the rear. Greg lived in one of the duplex units and rented out the other and the garage apartment. It proved an especially prescient move because Greg was yesterday's news when the sitcom flopped – and quite spectacularly at that – and he never worked as an actor again, unless voice-overs for feminine napkin commercials count as acting.

"I didn't know they still published books like these," Trace said.

"Are you kidding? He wrote one a month, twelve a year."

"Yes, Greg, I know how many months go into a year. For Christ's sake, how can you even think this was spontaneous combustion? It reeks of gasoline in here."

"I've owned this place for ten years, Trace. The apartment over the garage has always smelled like gasoline. That's why I gave him a break on the rent."

Trace moved to the bathroom. There was a large charred circle on the white tiled floor.

"Why didn't you put him out yourself?"

Greg nervously bit at a hangnail on an index finger. "I freaked, man. How often do you see people on fire? Plus I don't own a fire extinguisher."

"A garden hose?" Trace suggested with a raised eyebrow.

"Like I said, I freaked. I saw the fire, I ran up the stairs, and there he was on the bathroom floor, sitting cross-legged and all and burning like a fucking log. He wasn't screaming or nothing."

Trace leaned on his cane and carried himself back to the living room, back to that stack of smoldering gay porn novels.

"This is his suicide note," Trace announced.

"The faggot books?"

"Be nice."

Trace fumbled in his coat pocket for a pack of cigarettes, shook one loose, and lit it with a disposable lighter.

"I've had four books published and only one to this day continues to be a bestseller. You know what that one is? A book on sex positions. There are days when I wish I could burn every copy in existence."

"But you get residuals, don't you?"

"Not for that kind of writing."

Trace splurged for lunch at the H. Salt Fish and Chips on Lankershim Boulevard near Universal City. Between mouthfuls of deep fried whitefish and clams and zucchini strips Greg once again recounted the events of two nights before.

"I heard him leave about ten o'clock but then he came right back, like maybe less than ten minutes later. I was in the kitchen and the window looks out on the back so I saw him get out of the car and run up the stairs."

Greg drenched a plank of fish in malt vinegar. Trace left his gloves at home so he couldn't allow the acidic vinegar anywhere near his fingers.

"Anyway, I stayed in the kitchen, doing the dishes, and suddenly I heard this whoosh and then I go out – "

"Yeah, yeah, skip the rest. What did the fire department say about your theory?"

"They said he set himself on fire. But that's the thing, Trace, there's no gas can to be found anywhere and, like I said, the place always smells of gasoline. He was under a lot of stress. He was tired of writing these smut books and all – that's what he told me – and I think the pressure just got to him and – "

"He spontaneously combusted just like that. I see where you're going here, Greg. You want your little apartment house on the Graveline Tours or something, right? See the spot where a failed writer spontaneously combusted. And you want me to validate it for you."

"You're a writer. You can get the story into print."

"If it's true. Where's his car?"

"What?"

"You said he went out for about ten minutes before he went up in smoke. Where's his car?"

The silver Toyota Cressida was parked on the asphalt slab that passed for a driveway to the rear of Greg's house. The windows were rolled shut but the driver's side door was unlocked. Trace opened the door slowly, half expecting the car to be booby-trapped with some kind of incendiary device.

"Holy shit!" Trace hissed. "This thing is a gas can on wheels. Stick your fucking head in there."

Trace sat down on a cinder block in the driveway and rested. His legs were burning from the latest cruel permutation of his psoriasis; in fact, at this stage of the inflammation his skin resembled that of a burn victim and often confused doctors who were seeing him and his condition for the first time.

"You need anything, Trace?"

"Just to be home. Do you know where he went for ten minutes that night?"

"No idea."

"I do."

They drove in Greg's car a half a mile to a gas station on Laurel Canyon Boulevard near Gelson's Market. The station manager, an obscenely hirsute Persian with hair on every exposed surface of his skin, laughed long and hard when Trace began his inquiry.

"Let me see if I have this straight," Trace said as the man continued laughing at his recollection of events. "A man drives into your gas station at ten o'clock, walks up here to the window, pays for ten dollars worth of gasoline – "

"Yes, yes."

"And then he walks back to his car over there at the island and instead of putting the nozzle in his tank like most people, he takes a fucking shower in the shit and then calmly gets back into his car and leaves."

"Yes. Like I said, strange but funny."

"You didn't think of calling the police?"

The hairy Persian hiked his shoulders. "I wasn't here."

"Okay, fair enough. Your attendant didn't call the cops?"

"Why?" The man laughed again. "This is L.A. We'd have the police here all the time if we called them every time somebody did something…funny."

Iced Coffee

Trace considered Amy over the rim of his wine glass.

"If you told the guy that sleeping with you wouldn't advance his career, then you must've got the vibe that he wanted to sleep with you."

"He's in my class, Trace. He's a student of mine."

"Yeah, and he's got that young and handsomely Spanish thing that turns you on. Why did you two meet for coffee in the first place?"

"He said he had specific questions about a story of his that I read, that he didn't understand all my comments."

"And?" Trace lit a cigarette and studied her face through a swirl of blue smoke.

"And he didn't have specific questions, just sort of general writer-type questions: How do you organize your time? How did you get an agent? And he asked, 'Who did you meet at the conference in New York? Anybody worthwhile?' That was the vibe – plus he paid for my iced coffee."

"But you told him that sleeping with you – "

"I didn't exactly say sleeping with me wouldn't help him. I said sleeping with 'another writer' wouldn't help any of us. We need to sleep with editors and reviewers."

Amy laughed. Trace didn't.

She took a delicate sip of her wine and continued. "So he asked if I slept with any editors and reviewers and I replied 'Are any of my books bestsellers?' That was as much sexual banter as we engaged in. Honestly. I don't know what he wanted except to kiss me good-bye at the end, but it was too hot outside and I avoided even the hug."

"Is he a good writer?"

"He's a serious writer, spends a lot of time at it, reading and everything. But in terms of natural talent he's just not there."

"Uh, huh. Reminds me of the old joke about the Polish starlet who thought she could get ahead by sleeping with the writer."

"He's Spanish, not Polish."

"I think we're clear on that."

Rosebud

"I've got someone you have to meet, Trace. This guy is going to blow your mind. You won't believe the shit he owns."

The last time Trace encountered the dark-haired meth addict with restless hands he had tried to sell Trace on a wild, paranoid fantasy involving shadowy gunmen who were about to end his life.

"I'm glad to see you're still alive," Trace said. He sipped his Manhattan and scowled at the hotel bartender. Too much vermouth, not enough grenadine.

"Oh, man, don't listen to that shit I was spewing a few months ago. I was sick, man, I had a, you know, a whatchamacallit – "

"A brain tumor?"

"No, man." He laughed, loud and hard and nervous, a con artist thrown off his game. "It was like the flu."

"Like the flu?" Trace was amused. "So it was a twenty-four-hour bug or something? Made you think people were out to kill you?"

He settled onto the bar stool next to Trace and dipped his fidgety fingers into the bowl that held unpalatable snack foods, day-old bagel chips and corn chips slathered in dry chili powder.

"You need to meet this guy," he insisted. He ran a hand through his black hair and the fingers came back wet and slick. He plunged them back into the bowl of snacks, hair grease mingling with chili powder and stale bagel chips. He popped a handful into his mouth and chewed with open lips. "You ever see *Citizen Kane?*"

Trace recoiled from the sight of bagel chips crunching in his wet mouth and motioned to the bartender for a refill on his Manhattan.

"Of course I've seen *Citizen Kane*. Why? What of it?"

The meth head hopped off his stool as if he'd been shot through the ass by a rusty spring.

"Stay right here. Don't go away," he demanded and he scurried out of the bar like a man chasing his own shadow.

Trace had to go slow on the second cocktail. The new antidepressants his doctor had prescribed made his tolerance for alcohol lower than usual. Three drinks could easily put him under the table or – as in a scenario played out earlier that week with Amy – he could suddenly turn very frank and honest in conversation. The combination of Jack Daniels and Seroquel at lunch had amalgamated into a truth serum and he had blatantly asked Amy to stop dumping on him, stop using him as a sounding board for all the drama in her life and there was plenty of drama to be sure. Ordinarily he didn't mind listening to Amy's problems but at that particular alignment of mind and matter he was too preoccupied with his own mental health to swim in Amy's turbulent emotional waters.

The meth head returned in less than ten minutes; in tow was a short old man who cradled a bundle of some sort, wrapped in hotel towels, in his arms.

"This is Art," the meth head said by way of introduction. "Art is my neighbor here in the hotel."

At a longer gaze, Trace could see that the man was not old. He had been prematurely wizened and weathered by whatever his particular ravage was. Trace guessed it was alcohol. The man had rheumy eyes and dry white spittle at all four corners of his mouth, hemmed in by a thick five o'clock shadow. His short legs were unreliable toothpicks that threatened to snap at any moment and his plump belly was the cocktail olive that the toothpicks lanced through.

"Show him what you got, Art."

Art placed his bundle on the bar in front of Trace.

"Go ahead and open it," Art said to Trace. He cleared his throat to allow a pocket of phlegm the opportunity to disengage. He swallowed it back down when it hit his mouth. "But be careful. It's old."

"Well, it's larger than a bread box." Trace pushed his martini glass aside.

Trace gingerly folded back the stiff white hotel towels to reveal a child's sled, practically brand new. The runners and frame were of hard wood. The red seat was a furniture-quality wood composite with a carved logo and a black pinstripe border. The logo was one word: ROSEBUD.

"Do you recognize it?" the meth head asked expectantly.

"Yeah," Trace said, "It's a replica of the Rosebud sled from *Citizen Kane*. It's nice but so what?"

"It's not a replica," Art said. "My dad – "

"His dad worked on *Citizen Kane*, Trace. He was a prop whatchamacallit, a prop guy. Art has tales to tell, Trace. True stories about Orson Welles and shit."

"Uh, huh."

"Might make a good story, Trace. You could probably sell a good behind-the-scenes story about *Citizen Kane*, huh?"

Trace laughed. "That's a replica. You can buy them on eBay."

"It's the real deal, Trace."

"Is that what he told you?" Trace nodded to Art.

"Come on, Trace. Just talk to Art for a few minutes. Buy us a drink and talk to Art."

The bartender was now hovering nearby and paying close attention to the conversation.

"Two beers," Trace said dryly to the bartender. He turned back to the meth head. "And don't try to convince me that thing isn't a replica. For fuck sake, do you always go through this much song and dance for a drink?"

Blood and Wine

"I cried the day Ernest Gallo died," Mac confessed to Trace. "I sat right down on the edge of my bed with a bottle of Gallo wine and I cried like a baby."

Trace couldn't believe that his old friend consumed so much cheap wine and still managed to stay above ground. Mac's love for Gallo wine bordered on the romantic.

"A jug a day and Taco Bell, that's all I spend my money on, Trace."

The sparse furnishings in Mac's San Francisco apartment bore the truth of that statement. The living room played host to a threadbare brown sofa bed that smelled like a bus station men's room. That was it. No other furniture. The television was in Mac's bedroom, which was always kept under lock and key to keep the rats inside.

"Why do you have rats?"

Mac stood over the old four-burner gas stove in the kitchen and rubbed the stubble on his chin thoughtfully. He poured a tumbler full of Gallo Burgundy and thought about it a little more.

"I don't remember." And then he laughed, a high-pitched, throw-your-head-back cackle that exposed a row of uneven yellow teeth.

"Did you buy them at a pet store, Mac?"

Trace opened the pint bottle of Wild Turkey that he bought at the Safeway in the Marina District. He would drink straight from the neck of the bottle. He didn't trust any dishware in Mac's apartment. It was 1998. Trace was in San Francisco – the city of his birth

– for two days on assignment for *Hustler* magazine. He was writing a feature on German Nazi-era porn. The leading expert on the subject lived in San Francisco and refused a telephone interview. The magazine agreed to pay for Trace's travel but not accommodations.

"Leave early in the morning," his editor ordered, "and then turn around and drive back the same evening after you've done the interview."

Trace couldn't make such an arduous voyage in one day so he called his childhood friend.

"Sure, you can stay here," Mac said on the phone. "But I'm warning you in advance that my place is…well, it's usually a mess."

He had forgotten to warn Trace about the rats.

"They came with the apartment but I caught them in a cage and domesticated them. They're great pets, Trace."

"How do you domesticate a rat, Mac?"

Mac poured another slug of Gallo.

"Well, I never let them out of the bedroom, so in that regard is how I'm saying they're domesticated." He laughed again. Trace wanted to grab him by the lapels of that dirty, cum and piss stained cotton robe from Mervyn's and slam him against the wall.

"What the fuck have you done with your life?" Trace would have screamed at him. "You're a bum. You used to have talent."

When Trace and Mac Mayerling were growing up together in San Francisco they supported each other in their goals and ambitions. Trace wanted to be a reporter or a writer of some sort and Mac desired to illustrate album covers. Trace had never seen an artist with Mac's innate abilities. He could study any artist's work for a day or two and then sit down at an easel and exactly replicate the artist's style. If nothing else, Mac Mayerling could have become the world's greatest producer of art forgeries.

But something happened along the road to wishes and dreams fulfilled. For Trace, it took over a decade of toil before he would be allowed to call himself a professional, working writer. Along the way, he held down stints as a bar manager in San Francisco and San Diego, a security supervisor and stage manager at a Hollywood studio, and a development executive for a small production company with more ambition than cash in the bank.

What happened to Mac Mayerling, though, was a troubling mystery to Trace. He was a guitar craftsman for a spell and then fronted a punk rock band that played at low-rent venues throughout the Bay Area. He drank, too. A lot. And the drinking increased after Mac lost his parents within a year of each other. It would be too simple, Trace knew, to infer that the death of his parents spurred Mac Mayerling into a John O'Brien-styled drinking binge. According to the accounts of mutual friends, Mac was a functioning drunk before he hit thirty. He was now thirty-nine years old.

Trace returned to L.A. the next day with ninety minutes of prime interview material for his *Hustler* feature and a soul that was deeply disturbed by what had become of his friend. Mac had been working the last three years at a tie-dye T-shirt company in the Haight District.

"This is what you've done with your talent?" Trace confronted his friend. "You make T-shirts?"

Mac had shrugged his shoulders and laughed.

"I have full medical and dental," he said.

Trace slept that night on the sofa bed redolent in the odor of urine, listening in terror to the sound of rats trying to chew their way through the wall.

The first phone call came one month after Trace had visited Mac. When Trace answered the phone, Mac was in the middle of a full-force laughing fit.

"What's so goddamn funny, Mac?"

"I ... I – " Mac's breath came in shallow gasps between guffaws.

"Come on, Mac, it's late."

"I got arrested for a DUI!" Mac announced. "I was three times over the limit. I have to go to traffic school and they yanked my license for six months. Guess it's high time to buy a bike."

Trace's disappointment sunk in deeper but nothing prepared him for the next call.

"I had to have my annual physical for our health insurance carrier," Mac explained to Trace in a somber tone. "I was sweating bullets, man. I mean, you know, years of fucking drinking, I figured there had to be something wrong. Guess what I did? I just blurted out to the doctor 'I'm an alcoholic and I may have done damage to myself'!"

Mac laughed. "And so the doctor orders a series of tests, including a full liver panel and guess what?"

"You have cirrhosis."

"No!" Mac howled. "I'm perfectly fine, Trace. He said my liver was clean. He said there are some people whose bodies can tolerate any amount of alcohol abuse you can think of and that I might just be one of those people. Isn't that great?"

"Mac, listen to me. You have not been given a free license to drink all you want. You've actually been handed a warning."

Mac laughed, long and hard. Trace tried to get another word or two in edgewise but Mac's hyena-like screeching on the telephone was like line static from a madhouse.

Trace hung up and never spoke to Mac Mayerling again, though he did make a habit of scanning the obituary page of the *San Francisco Chronicle* every few months.

True Grit

Trace didn't know if there was a story to be found in the incident that occurred that hot summer evening on Wilshire Boulevard but it was a slow week and he had no work to speak of so he was willing to poke and paw and scrape until a properly melodramatic tale surfaced or until the facts revealed just another mundane and pointless two-paragraph piece that not even the AP wires would be interested in.

The bare facts were as follows: At approximately ten o'clock on a Friday evening, while Wilshire Boulevard was still alive with weekend traffic, revelers set free from their cubicles for forty-eight hours, Ulysses Pritchett, twenty-six, climbed atop the famous statue of John Wayne on horseback outside the Larry Flynt Tower at 8484 Wilshire Boulevard and leaped to the concrete pavement below. It was not a long fall but Pritchett was short and wiry, standing a mere five-foot-three when barefoot and weighing in at one hundred and ten pounds.

The statue was installed in 1979 when the high-rise office complex at Wilshire and La Cienega was home to Great Western Savings. The cowboy film star had been the financial institution's television spokesman. After his death from cancer, the board of directors figured they owed the larger-than-life American hero a fitting tribute, so the statue was commissioned and it still stood its mythic watch over the busy boulevard all these years later, long after Great Western had beat feet out of the building and Larry Flynt moved his Flynt Publications staff in.

Trace had been in the building on multiple occasions, always to pitch a story to one of *Hustler's* feature editors. He was impressed with the security. Flynt, the victim of an assassination attempt that left him paralyzed and wheelchair-bound – and many say drug-addled from the chronic pain – employed an internal security staff that would give the Secret Service a run for their money. Trace knew that Flynt Security would have good videotape of the incident from their bank of security monitors inside and outside the steel and glass edifice but he also knew that they would have turned those tapes over to the LAPD – not before producing their own dubs of the taped incident – and, in any event, would not give Trace the time of day. It had been years since he toiled for *Hustler* and the famous revolving door had ejected all of the editors he once worked with.

Wellbeck, Trace's contact within the Public Information Office of the L.A. County Coroner, told Trace over the phone that it would be weeks before a toxicology screen would be available to the public and the media.

"Off the record," Wellbeck said, "it looks like an accident. It was an uncontrolled fall."

An uncontrolled fall, Trace knew, could be fatal at very short distances. Such a tumble could result in massive head injury, torn liver and spleen, or shearing of the heart or the aorta. When Trace was a young boy in grade school he had an English teacher who succumbed to such a short and fatal fall while standing on a stepladder to replace a light bulb in her basement. It was one of his first encounters with death and it haunted Trace all of his life. She was an older woman, he recalled, with no husband and no family to speak of, a lonely English teacher in a small West Virginia town near the Ohio River, laid low by a light bulb and a simple stepladder purchased from a hardware store.

Outside an apartment building on La Cienega, mere blocks away from the Flynt Tower, Trace sat in his '48 Packard and rifled through a shoebox that contained all of his fake or long-expired press credentials. In L.A. it was easier to buy a handgun off the street than to get a sanctioned press pass from the Los Angeles Police Department, particularly after 9/11.

Gaining supervised entrance to Ulysses Pritchett's apartment was easier than Trace had imagined it would be. The apartment manager, a dowdy and middle-aged Armenian woman who smelled of fried onions and Dove soap, was impressed that a reporter from the *L.A. Times* would express interest in her young tenant's death. No one from the media, she assured Trace, had been snooping around the story at all.

"College student," she told Trace as they moved down the thinly carpeted corridor to Pritchett's seventh-floor apartment. "UCLA."

"Did he have a job?"

"Record store on Melrose," she said but was unable to recall the name of the store. She was sure she had it on file with his original rental application.

The apartment was neat and tidy. In the kitchen there was evidence of recent alcohol use: an open bottle of tequila on the tiled counter and sliced lime that had shriveled and become dried fruit in the forty-eight hours since Pritchett's fall from John Wayne.

"Girlfriend," the apartment manager said, pointing to a photograph of a lovely, raven-haired girl in a cheap picture frame that Ulysses probably picked up from one of the local 99 Cents stores.

"Do you know her?" Trace asked. The girl looked to be in her early twenties.

The woman shook her head. But she did know that her young tenant had a good friend who lived on the fourth floor.

Benny Medina answered the door of his apartment like he was expecting the hounds of Hell to greet him. His eyes were bloodshot from a mixture of tears and too much booze. Trace recognized the palsied shake in Medina's hands, one of the telltale signs of an alcoholic bender; that and the dirty clothes, unwashed skin, and the smell of sugar and rot in the unkempt, darkened apartment.

Trace flashed his fake *L.A. Times* press pass in Medina's face. Medina had to squint to recognize any object more than one foot away from his eyes. He was older than Pritchett, Trace could see, about thirty-five years old.

"Am I in trouble?" Medina asked Trace when he allowed him entrance to the apartment. He had told the Armenian manager to wait in the hallway, explaining to Trace that the two had a "blood feud."

"I'm half Turkish," Medina explained. "Goddamn Armenians think that the Turks tried a genocide number on them."

"Didn't they?" Trace said. He couldn't find a sofa or a chair in the filthy apartment that he felt comfortable sitting in so he remained standing amidst the piles of dirty clothes and old newspapers and grease-stained pizza boxes and fast food wrappers.

"You asked if you were in trouble. Why?"

"Well, you, uh, you said were here about Ulysses."

"Yes, I am."

Medina melted his thin frame into an armchair near the closed Venetian blinds on a balcony door that looked out on La Cienega. His unclean brown robe matched the chair's dirty upholstery perfectly. He splayed himself out sideways – one leg draped over the arm of the sofa, the other plopped on the floor. The foot resting on the floor twitched and tapped uncontrollably, motor impulses dancing to a song that Medina only heard in his head.

"Do you know about his girl?" Medina sighed.

"All I know is he took a header off the John Wayne statue in front of the Flynt building," Trace said flatly.

"There was this girl – "

"There always is," Trace said.

"He was really hung up on her, met her at school and all and they had been dating for a long time. They met every Tuesday and Thursday at this Italian place in the Village."

"Westwood Village?"

"Uh, huh."

"You said they were dating?"

"Yeah, man."

"Then why Tuesdays and Thursdays? That doesn't sound like much of a dating pattern to me."

"That's the point, man, that's what I'm getting to, okay? Cool?"

Trace nodded. Medina reached with a shaking hand for a small ceramic pot pipe on the beaten and slashed coffee table, a garage sale item if Trace ever saw one. Medina fired up the pipe with a red

Bic disposable lighter and sucked in a lungful of smoke, offering the pipe to Trace.

"No, thanks. So Tuesdays and Thursdays?"

"Yeah, that's when they met and then one day he finds out – this is after they've been seeing each other for, like, six months or something like that – "

"On Tuesdays and Thursdays – "

Medina was getting rattled. "That's what I said, man."

"Let me see if I can finish the story for you," Trace said. "He found out she was married."

Medina exhaled a plume of smoke and regarded Trace like an oracle.

"I thought you didn't know anything about her. What're you, like, a Psychic Hotline guy or something?"

Medina laughed.

"No, it's just common sense. A woman who is only available certain days of the week, probably days when her husband is out of town or when he thinks she's attending a class at school – a story like that always has the same ending. How did he feel when he found out?"

"At first he was really pissed," Medina said, packing fresh weed into the pipe. "But then he got in a real funk. Night before last it was really bad. I was up at his place and we were shooting the shit and stuff – "

"And knocking back tequila shooters?" Trace said.

Medina laughed again, a ridiculous, almost child-like chortle.

"Yeah, tequila shooters 'til about a quarter to nine and then I had to go home but we had been talking the shit for hours and I was trying to make him feel better, you know? I didn't mean to say what I said."

Trace shifted on his feet uncomfortably, like a boxer trying to dance around a head blow that he knew was coming. He wanted a cigarette but he didn't want to contribute to the stale, damp, and oppressive air in the apartment.

"What did you say, Benny?"

"Well, I'd been telling him that he should just tell her to fuck off and that there's other fish in the sea and all."

"Sage advice."

"And then – "

Medina couldn't stand recalling it without a shot of tequila himself. He reached for a pint bottle of Jose Cuervo on the coffee table, drinking straight from the neck of the bottle, spilling a little bit on his bathrobe.

"It was just as I was leaving, going out the door."

"Okay – " Now it was Trace who was growing rattled and impatient.

"Well, he always liked John Wayne and cowboy movies and stuff – he was from Oklahoma, you know – and he liked that John Wayne statue down the street so I told him – I told him, man, I said, 'Ulysses, you need to be just like John Wayne and jump back in the saddle and ride again, son.' That's what I said. Get back in the saddle and ride again."

"And then you left him alone?"

"Yeah, man." He was close to tears then. "I didn't think the stupid fucker would take me literally."

Swimming to Acapulco

It was 3:45 on a mild Thursday afternoon and Acapulco was beckoning Trace (the chain restaurant, not the actual Mexican resort, which Trace had never been to) so into his briefcase went the research file on his new magazine assignment and a paperback copy of *The Stories of John Cheever.*

And he was out the door.

As usual and without disappointment, the "cantina" was empty when Trace arrived except for the bartender, a thin and wiry young Mexican-American who disquietly called all the male patrons "Boss."

"Do you want some appetizers today, Boss? Some guacamole or some buffalo wings?"

"No, thanks, just the margarita for now."

"Okay, Boss."

Trace perused through the research file casually, made a few pertinent notes, and pulled the six-hundred-and-ninety-three-page volume of Cheever short stories out of his battered briefcase.

He began reading 'The Swimmer,' which he wanted to read immensely in the quiet of the bar, away from the confines of his combination home and office, and he began with the now-classic opening line:

> It was one of those midsummer Sundays when everyone sits around saying, 'I drank too much last night.'

Just as Trace finished the line that pulls the reader into the story from the starting gate, Sharif arrived. Like the character of Neddy Merrill in Cheever's 'The Swimmer,' Sharif was something of a living ghost but what he haunted were barstools around Glendale. Not that Sharif – who owned a lucrative dressmaking business – was a drunk. Far from it. The thin, dark-skinned, Egyptian-born businessman sipped Courvoisier all day long and conducted business over his cell phone.

He saddled up on the stool right next to Trace.

"Where is your woman? The one you used to come here with?" Sharif inquired in his deep and petroleum-thick accent after he ordered his brandy with water back.

It was apropos of nothing as Sharif and Trace rarely exchanged more than a polite "Hello."

"Which one?" Trace siphoned some margarita from the glass before him with a blue straw. It tasted like an alcohol-laced Slurpee.

"Dark hair and – " He cupped two half-fists to his chest to complete the sentence: Dark hair and big tits.

"She doesn't live here anymore," Trace replied, bored, anxious to get back to Neddy's horrific progress from optimism to bottomless despair as he made a symbolic cross-county swim from one affluent swimming pool to another.

"Oh," Sharif said and took a slow sip from his brandy snifter.

Hero's Journey

Trace was picking up so many talismans lately that he was beginning to feel like a mythical hero on a journey that someone else was writing.

The best prize so far was the canvas Jack London book bag he found at the local Barnes and Noble the day after U.C. Berkeley acquired his essay on Jack London and Teddy Roosevelt. The strangest talisman was the actual talisman that his demented fan Gloria sent him for "good luck."

"It worries me when psycho stalkers begin wishing me good luck," he told his former agent, Ray, over lunch in the hotel restaurant.

Trace and Ray were dancing around the subject of Ray possibly taking Trace on as a client again. Three years earlier, Ray, a relative newcomer to the world of literary representation, shepherded and encouraged Trace's urban thriller screenplay *Claws*. When the requisite rewrites and revisions and polishes were finished Ray was ready to, as they say, "take it out."

"I need to give it to some trusted confidantes to read first," Ray announced three days before he was ready to take the script out all over town. "For feedback, that's all."

The feedback that Ray required from the three "confidantes" was not what he expected. The screenplay was good, yes, but it was going to be a hard sell for many reasons, they told him. There was the problem, for instance, with the lead character, a black animal control officer from South Central L.A.

"The character sounds too black," one of Ray's colleagues complained.

Another colleague, who worked in a development capacity for rapper Ice Cube's production company, moaned that the protagonist "didn't sound black enough."

Ray sounded bereaved on the telephone when he called Trace to inform him that, based on the feedback he received, he couldn't take the screenplay out.

What Trace discovered over the ensuing days was that the three "confidantes" and "colleagues" of Ray's were actually his sole connections in the business, the only people in town who would read a screenplay represented by Ray Wilkinson Management.

Trace howled, wrote incendiary letters to Ray, spoke to a lawyer who informed him that the agent had violated a trust, and once pondered murdering the bastard in some spectacular fashion that would have talent agents around town treating writers with nothing but trembling respect for the rest of their pathetic days.

Now, three years later, the scorched earth was beginning to heal, as charred soil will do, and Ray wanted to know if Trace would consider being represented by Ray Wilkinson Management once more.

Trace was still thinking about it when the waitress brought the check. Ray reached inside his jacket and extracted one of his prized possessions, a Parker 100 fountain pen, and scribbled his signature on the credit card receipt.

"I just had an idea," Trace said, retrieving a notebook from his canvas bag on the floor. "Some thoughts on how we might work together."

Trace reached across the table and plucked the pen from Ray's fingers and began writing hastily in the notebook. What he was writing was gibberish, wasting time until Ray's cell phone would inevitably chirp and he would step away from the table to take the call.

Within five minutes Ray's cell phone chimed and Ray politely and customarily excused himself to confab with whatever writer he was going to screw over next.

Trace dropped the Parker pen into his Jack London bag and when Ray returned to the table he suddenly feigned urgency.

"I've really got to get going, Ray," Trace said, getting to his feet quickly. "I'll call you later in the week."

He briskly walked out of the hotel restaurant.

Another talisman.

On The Road to Rockville

"Poor sonofabitch."

"What did you say?"

"Poor sonofabitch." The Meth head tapped the cover of *The Great Gatsby* that rested on the bar top next to Trace's mug of beer. "That's what Dorothy Parker said at his funeral."

"Actually, it wasn't at his funeral she said that," Trace corrected. "It was when she went to view Fitzgerald's body at the mortuary in Culver City, before he was shipped back to Rockville for burial."

"Yeah, I knew that." He caught the hotel bartender's eye and gestured to the beer tap. "A short one, please."

Trace stared at his friend, amazed. "How did you know that about Dorothy Parker?"

"C'mon, Trace, just because I'm all fucked up on drugs these days doesn't make me a complete goddamn idiot, though my ex-wife would say otherwise but we're not asking her so fuck the bitch where she breathes."

"Give him a bourbon on the rocks," Trace instructed the bartender. "It's on me."

Trace sipped his beer and stared at the cover of the First Edition Library copy of *The Great Gatsby* in front of him. It was an authentic, hardcover reproduction of the original 1925 dust jacket by artist Francis Cugat, a haunting painting of the fantastic and desolate billboard alongside the railroad track between West Egg and New York, the eyes of Dr. T. J. Eckleburg, Optometrist.

"You ever think of getting into a program?" Trace asked his friend.

"You ever think of adopting a sunny disposition, Trace?"

Trace laughed. "My ex-wife Gina used to call me a pessimist. I always shot back that I'm a realist."

"Same difference." The bartender delivered his bourbon on the rocks and he tried hard to pretend that he didn't want to knock it back in one big gulp. "How come you never asked my name?"

"How come you never volunteered it?"

"Archie." He thrust a trembling hand toward Trace, the look on his face daring him to accept it. Trace ran his palm along the crease of his Levi's and shook Archie's moist hand.

"Pleased to meet you, Archie."

"So what's with Fitzgerald? Just a little reading matter or something bigger? You writing something?"

"Trying to. But I can't interest any editors so far. I want to do a first-person piece for a magazine. I want to go to Rockville and get drunk on Fitzgerald's grave. I met this guy in a bar on Hollywood Boulevard one day – "

"You sure do hang out in bars a lot."

Trace ignored the comment. "Anyway, I stopped in for a beer and I had a copy of *Gatsby* with me."

"Do you always bring reading material to bars? Doesn't that inhibit the social process?"

"Quite the opposite, Archie. It's a sure conversation starter. Just like you started a conversation when you saw the book on the bar there."

"I was fishing for a drink," Archie said with a smile. "Sorry. Continue."

"So, I'm sitting there having a Red Hook and leafing through *Gatsby*, trying to remember what it was old Owl Eyes says at Gatsby's funeral – "

"Poor sonofabitch," Archie repeated. "Same thing Dorothy Parker said."

"Uh, huh. So there's a guy sitting there, kind of a nondescript fellow, around thirty maybe, and we start talking about Fitzgerald and it turns out this guy went to Richard Montgomery High School, which is in Rockville, Maryland, right off a major road called Rockville Pike."

"Wasn't there a novel called *Rockville Pike*?"

"Yes, by Susan Coll. Jeez, can I finish this story?"

"I'm sorry, Trace. Go ahead."

Trace fumbled in the canvas carryall bag at his feet until he found his wire-bound memo book. He leafed through it manically until he found the tattered pages carrying his hastily drawn notes.

"On one side of the pike there's the high school campus, this guy tells me. If you walk up the campus and cross the pike, there's a very small church on a very, very small hill." He checked his notes for a moment before proceeding. "To the left of the church there's a small graveyard on the hill. It's not protected by any gates or stone wall or anything. You can just walk up in it. All the gravestones are small, he tells me, except for one towards the back center. It towers above all the others, and that's Fitzgerald's. The headstone stands up in the traditional upside down U-shape, and then a slab of stone lays flat with an inscription from *Gatsby*. Scott and Zelda's names are on the headstone."

Trace finished his beer and nodded to the bartender for a refill.

"Here's the thing, Archie, here's the fucking story, okay? His creative writing teacher used to take the class to write by the stone sometimes when the weather was nice. He said all the kids that were into literature were fascinated to have his stone right there; so whenever they passed through the graveyard – which was pretty often, since the shortcut from the school to the subway station was directly through the graveyard – they would leave a token of esteem, a cigarette or a joint or sometimes they'd plan ahead and get him a bottle of something. He said they assumed other kids took them as they passed as needed, and left their own gifts when they could."

Archie stared at Trace blankly. "I'm sorry. I don't see the story here."

"What? Kids leaving joints and bottles of gin on Fitzgerald's headstone? You don't see the story? You're as bad as the editors I've been pitching to."

Archie took a sip of the amber bourbon on ice and savored the taste in his mouth. He swallowed slowly and chewed on an ice cube thoughtfully.

"Yeah, well, that's the thing about me that you probably never would've guessed, Trace."

"What thing?"

Archie flashed a crooked smile. "I used to be an editor, men's magazines mostly, Busty Beauties kind of shit, but, yeah, I used to be an editor."

For the second time Trace gazed at his friend in silent astonishment.

"Do you mind if I ask what happened?"

Archie didn't hold back with the bourbon now. He downed it in one brave, throat-scorching swallow.

"Gotta quote Fitzgerald to answer that one, Trace." Archie rolled his eyes in the back of his head as if the words might be tattooed on his eyelids. "When we are in our thirties we want friends. In our forties we know that they won't save us any more than love did."

Archie gently replaced the empty glass on the barstool. There was meaning in that gesture, Trace knew, some vague gallantry, a momentary recollection of better days behind and probably a premonition of darker days ahead.

"Thanks for the drink, Trace."

"Monkeys on Sunset Boulevard" A Dan Knight Story

"You cannot have an affair with this woman," she insisted.

Dan took his large coffee from the Starbucks barista and moved to the little counter where the sugar and cream was kept. Susan dogged his heels, refusing his offer of coffee or tea. She avoided all caffeinated beverages.

"It will ruin your career, what little of one you have," Susan continued. "I'm not berating you, Dan, I'm stating a fact."

Dan smiled demurely and stirred the cream and sugar into his coffee with a wooden swizzle stick. "Patio?"

Outside, mid-morning traffic roared by on Sunset Boulevard. Dan took a seat under an umbrella at a plastic table. Susan joined him with a heavy sigh.

"I'm not just your agent, I'm your friend, Dan. And I'm telling you this woman is dangerous."

"I think I'm in love with her."

"She's married. And not just that, but married to one of the most powerful producers in this town. Does she think she's in love with you?"

Dan hiked his shoulders carelessly. "I don't know. I've never asked her."

"Oh, Jesus, Dan. What're you getting into? People are starting to talk."

"Let them talk. I don't care. We're just friends."

Susan fished in her handbag for a pack of smokes. "Just friends? I thought you just said you thought you were in love with her."

"Is there a point to all of this, Susan?"

"A point?" She lit up a cigarette with a slender gold lighter. "Fuck, yes, there's a point. You start screwing around with this woman and your writing career is dead in the water. As it is you only have two TV credits."

"And uncredited rewrites on two features," Dan pushed back. "Besides, do you think her husband is the only producer in town?"

"Of course not. Just the most connected."

Dan pawed a hand in the air as if swatting a fly. Susan had never seen him acting so recklessly.

"Let me tell you a story."

Dan laughed. "Isn't that my job?"

"Not this time." She flicked cigarette ash onto the hot pavement and crossed her left leg over her right. Dan noticed her thighs for the first time. They were creamy with a wild varicose vein tracing the upper thigh of her left leg.

"A few years ago in India," she began, "a farmer got annoyed by a monkey that had made a home in one of his trees. So what does he do? He grabs his shotgun and takes a shot at the monkey, meaning to scare him off."

"Is this a true story?"

"Yup. Heard it on NPR. So, anyway, he means to just scare the monkey off but instead he accidentally shoots and kills her – and she was nursing a baby at the time."

"A baby monkey?" Dan sipped his coffee casually.

"Of course a baby monkey. So, the Indian police arrest the farmer for shooting an endangered species. They try to get the baby monkey but he won't let go of his dead mama. So they drag both dead mom and the baby into the police station along with the farmer while they try to figure out how to handle the situation."

"One big happy family." Dan smiled. She hated him when he was being smug.

"They're all sitting there trying to figure out what to do and you know what happens next? Monkeys. Dozens of them. They converge on the police station. They climb on the roof, others surround the building."

Susan bit down on the last sentence and allowed the words to hang in the air as if they contained some special meaning.

"And…?"

"And, according to the news report that I heard, while the dozens of monkeys are surrounding the station, two of them break from the pack and quietly enter the station and make off with the baby."

"Jesus. This is true?"

"One hundred percent true. Why would NPR make up such a thing? So – "

"So you're saying there's a lot of monkeys in this town."

Patchen Pass

"I'm not going to your sister's funeral," Trace's father announced with abrupt finality.

Trace fumbled with the cell phone as he slipped into a black Van Heusen dress shirt. Jesus, he fumed to himself, you'd think the man had been asked to remove one of his own testicles with a blunt kitchen knife instead of attending the funeral of his only daughter.

"Is Mom going?" Trace asked. He hastily buttoned the shirt and began searching for a suitable necktie.

"Your mother can do whatever she wants. She always does."

With that as his final statement, Trace's father hung up the phone. It wasn't a rude gesture. He was that way his whole life. He simply didn't believe in saying good-bye.

There was no way Trace could ask the Packard to endure the long drive from L.A. to Santa Clara. The water pump would give out before he made it over the Grapevine. Flying was also out of the question. Trace ceased all commercial air travel after he wrote a magazine exposé on the February 2000 crash of Alaska Airlines Flight 261. That lack of effective lubrication on a simple goddamn jackscrew could bring down an airplane, killing everyone onboard, was a concept that horrified him.

Trace opted for Amtrak. It was the only option remaining, aside from Greyhound. He boarded the train at the Burbank station and immediately hit the bar. By the time he was on his sixth scotch and water, legs stretched out on the empty seat across from him as he watched the bland farmland of Kern County roll by, he started to miss his sister Lynn.

The news of Lynn's death hadn't come as a surprise. She was a drug addict most of her adult life, which ended now at the age of forty-five. She was a non-discriminating user, imbibing whatever was affordable at the moment and affordable in mass quantities. Pot, speed, meth, coke, pills of every stripe. Someone told Trace she even snorted heroin a few times.

Everyone knew that drugs would eventually bring Lynn down but no one could have foreseen the awful circumstances, the grim scenario that awaited Trace's sister.

The rain had been steady and heavy that year in the Santa Cruz Mountains, leaving the soil unreliable. Lynn hiked the mountains once a week with two Hefty garbage bags in tow. She collected discarded plastic and aluminum bottles to take to the recycling center near her apartment in Santa Clara. Collecting recyclables was her only form of income, the only way to pay for the narcotic stupor she remained in every waking hour of the day and night.

According to the mountain rescue team that retrieved her body, Lynn had parked her Toyota pick-up at the summit of Highway 17 near Patchen Pass. She probably stepped out on a precipice of what appeared to be solid earth to retrieve a can or bottle and the mud gave way beneath her Birkenstock-clad feet, sending her plummeting 1,808 feet to her death in the canyon below.

"It's going to be a closed casket," Trace's mother chirped as a greeting when she met him at the San Jose Amtrak station.

"Hello to you, too, Mom," Trace grumbled, slinging the strap of his garment bag over his shoulder and walking in step with her toward the parking lot. Trace felt nothing but animus toward his mother his entire life and he figured his feelings would remain that way until he took a last, fatal step into the void like Lynn did.

A hell of a way to get away from mom, he thought.

In the car on the way to the funeral home Trace announced that he would like to write and deliver the eulogy at Lynn's service.

Trace's mother clucked her tongue and shook her head slowly. "Do you really think that's such a good idea, Trace?"

"I've already made some notes," Trace said, pulling the sixty-sheet wire-bound memo notebook from his hip pocket.

"You know what I mean," she said, plowing through a yellow light on El Camino Real.

"I don't write for magazines like that anymore, Mom."

"But everyone who will be there knows that you did."

"Why?" Trace snapped. "Because you told them?"

"I really wish you had started your career somewhere else," his mother sighed.

"I started where I started," Trace said between gnashed teeth, shoving the notebook back into his pocket. "A lot of decent writers started out in the men's magazine racket."

"In any event, I just don't think it would be right. I asked the funeral home director to deliver the sermon and eulogy. I gave him all the pertinent facts of Lynn's life and he's going to write something up. I'm sure it will be nice."

They drove in silence the rest of the way.

It was overcast the day of Lynn's memorial service. Trace saw family members that he hadn't laid eyes on in decades and he made little effort to renew their acquaintance. He took his place in the front pew next to his mother and longed for a drink and a cigarette.

"Lynn loved nature," the gaunt funeral home director announced as he launched into his eulogy. "Her devotion to nature was exhibited fully in her death."

Trace squirmed on the hard bench of polished wood.

"The day that Lynn died," the eulogist who never knew Lynn continued, "she was in the mountains collecting trash, helping to keep nature beautiful and unsoiled."

It took every ounce of energy Trace had to keep from laughing hysterically. But later that night, ensconced in his room at the Kings Highway Motel with a bottle of Jack Daniels, he laughed until he cried.

Stalked

"Hi."

"Hello."

"Did you just get here?"

"No. I've been here for about a half hour. I had an appointment in Beverly Hills at eleven and it broke up early."

"Oh, that's too bad."

"What is?"

"That your meeting broke up early."

"It was no big deal, hon. I mean, it doesn't mean anything bad happened."

"I wasn't implying that, Trace."

"I know."

"Then why – never mind. Did you just call me 'hon'?"

"Yes."

"I thought we were past that."

"Is that what you wanted to talk about? It's a fucking term of endearment, Amy. Get over it."

"You're gonna get hostile now?"

"What? What the fuck? Can we start over again, please? Hello, how was the traffic on the way over? Would you like to see a menu, Wags?"

Trace waited a beat and proceeded. "So I got a box in the mail from her the other day. Priority Mail."

"From who? Your stalker?"

"Yup."

"I don't get it. I've had four novels published and I've never had a stalker. You've published one successful book and you have a stalker and how many obsessive fans?"

"Who's counting?"

Amy laughed. "I don't mean to laugh. It's actually very scary."

"Tell me about it. I'm flagging the waitress for another beer. Do you want another Merlot?"

"Yeah, sure. Did you open the box?"

"Of course I did. Only after putting it out on the balcony and kicking it a few times to make sure there were no living creatures inside of it."

"Jesus, Trace. Maybe you should've just returned it?"

"And risk pissing her off? No way."

"I thought you said she's in Ohio, though."

"What? You never heard of air travel?"

"What was in the box?"

Trace lit a cigarette. The trendy little eatery on Santa Monica Boulevard in West Hollywood allowed smoking on the outdoor patio. Soon, Trace knew, cigarette smoking would be banned damn near everywhere except in your own home. They were already doing it in the City of Santa Monica. Day by day, little freedoms being stripped away.

"There was all kinds of shit inside, every item hand picked to show me how much research she has done on me."

"Fuck."

"Remember that tiger screenplay I wrote?"

"Of course."

"There was a tiger coffee mug, a Barnum and Bailey circus souvenir kind of thing. And then there was a book about vampires with a bookmark placed in it to a picture of John Holmes as a vampire."

"Because of the article you wrote about Holmes – "

"And because of a book review I wrote of the new edition of Bram Stoker's *Dracula*."

"Fuck. What else?"

"Fruit crate labels. You know how I collect those, right? I used to buy them on eBay. So she sent fruit crate labels to demonstrate that she had tracked my eBay purchases."

"This is getting scary."

Trace exhaled a thick plume of smoke. "And then there was a motel room key. The Pioneer Inn on Kini Island in Oshkosh, Wisconsin."

"Oshkosh, Wisconsin?"

"Don't ask me to figure all of it out, Wags, she's just fucking nuts, okay?"

"Have you talked to the police?"

"Nothing they can do."

"A restraining order?"

"Can't afford the lawyer to get it done right."

"Was there a note or anything like that in the box?"

"Nope. Nothing. I haven't even got to the weird part."

"There's a weird part?"

"At the bottom of the box were all these old film reels from the Seventies. Old stag films."

"Representing your days in porno – "

"Well, it's not exactly a secret."

Amy sipped her Merlot while Trace finished his cigarette.

"I think I should move," he finally said, crushing out the cigarette on the heel of his shoe with more aggression, Amy noted, than necessary.

Hypergraphia

The voice on the telephone was sharp and insistent, but Trace couldn't hear what the man was saying because he was still half asleep and was holding the receiver upside down. He suddenly recalled a Chandler novel that started this way, a sleepy-eyed Phillip Marlowe receiving an early morning phone call from a stranger. And everything goes wrong after that.

"Can you hear me, Trace? It's Greg. You have got to get over here and see this."

It was no stranger after all. It was Greg Harrington, an old friend, failed sitcom actor turned landlord. He owned a modest home in North Hollywood with rental properties in the rear and another apartment for lease above the garage. It was in the garage apartment a few months before that Greg lost one of his tenants to self-immolation, a stunt that Greg, at the time, mistook for a case of spontaneous combustion until Trace proved it was suicide.

Trace flipped the phone around and fumbled on the nightstand for a pack of cigarettes.

"I can hear you now. What goddamn time is it, Greg?"

"It's 7:30. Will you please come over? I can't even begin to describe this."

Trace lit a cigarette and raised up in bed on one elbow. "Try. Start at the beginning."

"One of my tenants died last night."

"Another one? How did this one off himself?"

"Heart attack, that's what the paramedics say. You should've seen the guy, Trace. He'd really lost it in the last few months, became a hermit and packed on about two hundred pounds. There were empty donut boxes all over the place, looked like that was all he ever ate."

Trace staggered to the microwave and nuked a mug full of water for instant coffee.

"Fat guy eats a lot of donuts and has a coronary. Tell me why this is interesting to me, Greg, let alone compelling enough to drag me out of bed on a hot goddamn Sunday morning."

"He has no family. That's what he told me. So I have to get rid of all of his stuff myself. And I think there's something here you need to see, Trace."

Trace poured two teaspoons of Folgers Instant into the cup of steaming water. "Okay. The suspense is killing me. I'll be there in two hours."

"Two hours?" Greg protested. "You're a fifteen-minute drive away."

"That's right." Trace hung up the phone. He had another cigarette with his coffee and then sat down at the keyboard. He had two hundred and fifty words to write before breakfast, a slam-dunk piece for an online literary journal about how *The Great Gatsby* influenced him or otherwise changed his life. At least ten other writers had also been asked to contribute short essays. He wrote quickly, a cigarette dangling from the corner of his mouth:

"The drive to Yosemite National Park the summer of 1972 was, as usual, fraught with danger because my stepfather had been drinking again. When Bobby began drinking all of the ghosts of Vietnam slithered out of their graves and encouraged him to sadistic and suicidal actions, such as taking hairpin mountain curves in our family station wagon at seventy miles per hour. He took glee in the terror that invoked in the family – my mom, my younger sister, and me.

"I was twelve years old that summer. Sometimes when Bobby would pull into a mountain pass at breakneck speed I would close my eyes and pretend I was on a rickety roller coaster and pray for straightaway roads. The rest of the time I kept my nose buried in a dog-eared paperback of *The Great Gatsby*. I absorbed all two hundred and eighteen pages of that lush novel during the drive from San Francisco to Yosemite and heaved a sigh of relief when we made it to the park in one piece. No station wagon crumpled in a heap over the side of a mountain. Limbs and life intact, mental faculties sorely compromised.

"Late that first night, staring at the majesty of Half Dome under a full moon, my young mind contemplated Fitzgerald's tale of delusional love and I wondered what it would be like to pine for another man's wife. Decades later, as I grew into a man, I would be accused of suffering from White Knight Syndrome, a need to 'rescue' women in perilous situations – usually bad marriages.

"And I am frightened by mountain roads to this day."

It took Trace less than ten minutes to pound out the two hundred and fifty words. He did a quick spell check and then e-mailed the document to the editor of the journal. There was no money to be made from the effort but anything that kept his name alive and out there was just fine with Trace.

Two hours later he was standing in a cramped and dark apartment in North Hollywood that once belonged to a fat man with a fetish for Winchell's Donuts.

"It stinks in here," Trace complained. "Open a fucking window, will ya?"

"I'm sorry," Greg said solicitously, cracking open one of the windows. "He'd been dead for three days before anyone knew about it. One of the neighbors told me she was worried about him and I used the master key to let myself in and I found him there – "

He pointed to a small writing desk in a corner of the apartment. On the desk were stacks of journals and loose-leaf notebooks.

"He was slumped over the desk," Greg explained, "and he still had a pen in his hand."

Trace picked up one of the notebooks and opened it. The scrawl was small and childish and cramped on the pages inside like so many monkeys jammed into a cage at the zoo.

"There are notebooks everywhere," Greg said excitedly. He opened an old two-drawer steel filing cabinet to reveal dozens upon dozens of spiral, loose-leaf notebooks, each one filled from front to back with handwritten words.

"I read some of it last night, Trace. It's not bad. He was writing a book, apparently."

"He was writing something," Trace agreed.

Greg had somehow convinced himself that the dead man might be the next John Kennedy Toole, the overhyped novelist whose book *A Confederacy of Dunces* became a cult classic after the author's untimely death.

"There might be something here, Trace."

"And if there is, what are you suggesting we do, Greg? Steal his material?"

"No way, man. You know me. I'm more ethical than that. But you know publishers and people like that. We can be credited as the guys who discovered him, you know?"

Trace shoved ten of the notebooks – grabbed at random – into a paper bag and promised he would have a read and render a verdict. He trusted Greg's instinct for literary material like he trusted those wingnuts in the Pentagon to leave well enough alone in the Middle East.

Late that night, Trace settled in with a bottle of Jack Daniels and the stack of notebooks. Many of the pages were flecked with grease and dried powdered sugar. The man's name, Oswald McKenna, was written in neat scrawl on the cover of every notebook. On the inside cover of all the notebooks were two simple words: *For Cecilia.*

By two in the morning, Trace was bleary-eyed and half in the bag from the Jack Daniels and too much bad prose. The book started out as a journey into magical realism, the tale of a coyote in the Hollywood Hills who shape shifts into a human and infiltrates the home of a wealthy record producer. It wasn't bad. It was awful. The writing was, at best, rambling and incoherent, manic and frenzied, words being spilled for their own sake, for the price of the ink, for the justification of the notebook and the paper, a mind cluttered with words like Trace imagined a mathematician's mind must be jammed with numbers and equations.

"How old was this Oswald McKenna?" Trace asked Greg the next morning.

"I don't know. Mid-fifties. Trace, there must be around four hundred notebooks here and check this out – I let him use a storage locker above the garage. Well, I opened it this morning and you'll never guess what I found."

"Notebooks," Trace said quickly. "Hundreds of them. Do you know anything about his personal life, like a girl named Cecilia in particular?"

"Nothing. He was a private guy."

"Okay, let's try something simple: Where did he work?"

Work for Oswald McKenna was a clerk's job at the Barnes and Noble bookstore in the Media Center Mall in Burbank. When Trace located the manager of the store, he flashed his fake *L.A. Times* press credential in his face.

"We were wondering what happened to him when he didn't show for work for five days," the manager said. "He loved his job so I didn't think he would quit without saying something."

"Heart attacks have a way of silencing people," Trace said. "We're trying to locate the next of kin, in particular a woman named Cecilia. Does that ring a bell?"

The manager searched his brain for a moment and then shook his head. "Oswald was a pretty private guy. Good with the customers, knew a lot about books, fiction was his specialty. He did his job and during breaks he sat over in the coffee shop and wrote in a notebook. Same routine every day."

"Really? How long had he been working here?"

"Three years."

"And you saw him writing in a notebook every day for three years?"

"Like I said, it was his routine: coffee, a donut or a muffin, and his notebook. We used to call him The Scribbler behind his back but we didn't mean anything cruel by it. Oswald was a cool guy.

He'd been putting on a lot of weight recently, though, so the heart attack makes a lot of sense."

"We have a little problem here, Ken." Trace read the manager's name off his lapel badge. "Oswald left some...unique items behind and we're trying to find anyone who may resemble next of kin. Would you happen to have his original job application still on file?"

Trace's hunch paid off in spades. Cecilia was Cecilia Sharpe of Culver City, her address and telephone number listed as Oswald McKenna's emergency contact.

When Trace knocked on the door of the modest bungalow in Culver City that afternoon he wasn't certain why he was there. The woman who answered the door and identified herself as Cecilia Sharpe was a frumpish woman in her early sixties. Her eyes were slate gray and there were still blonde roots in the gray hair that matched her eyes. There was a slight tremble in her lower lip and right hand that mimicked the early stages of Parkinson's.

"I haven't heard Oswald's name in years," she said when she invited Trace in for tea. "You say he left me something?"

"A lot of something, Miss Sharpe."

Trace sat down on a sofa that smelled of mothballs and cat litter. When she offered him a nip of blackberry wine in his tea he graciously accepted.

"Oswald liked to write, Miss Sharpe."

"Oh, my. Did he ever. He always wanted to be a writer."

"Well, there's a big difference between the craft of writing and the physical act of writing."

Cecilia Sharpe furrowed her brow, lost in the meaning of Trace's words.

"From what I can tell, Miss Sharpe, Oswald suffered from a mental problem called hypergraphia – that's a compulsion to write. It's caused by a problem in the brain's circuitry."

"Maybe. But he was still a writer."

"Had he ever been published?"

"Not to my knowledge, no. Perhaps, though, I owe you an explanation."

Cornelia Sharpe met Oswald McKenna, she explained, when they were both in their twenties. She was a waitress at a dive bar on the Sunset Strip and Oswald was an aspiring writer who filled the time between dreams bussing tables. They dated casually – at least as far as Cecilia was concerned, it was casual dating – but Oswald fell hard for her.

"He asked me to marry him on our third date. I didn't know what to say to that. I barely knew the man. So I made him a vow."

"A vow?"

"I told Oswald that if he ever wrote a book that landed on the *New York Times* bestseller list I would marry him immediately."

"I think he took that vow very seriously, Miss Sharpe."

The following morning Trace rented a pick-up truck from the local U-Haul dealer. He and Greg carefully packed the six hundred notebooks into the bed of the truck.

"This is insane," Greg said to Trace. "Thirty some-odd years of writing in the hopes that this woman – "

"Gatsby had his light at the end of the pier," Trace said. "We all need a light at the end of the pier, no matter how goddamn elusive or misguided the quest."

"Does she really want all this shit?"

Trace heaved a sigh. "She wept when I told her about it, okay? That's all I know and, yes, she said she would take the notebooks."

They lifted the last box into the truck and Trace slid behind the wheel.

"Do me a favor, Greg. Next time one of your tenants dies – keep it to yourself, okay?"

The Poet and the Pistolero

New Colombia was a small fishing village south of Ensenada, Mexico, and far north of anywhere Trace ever wanted to be. All that is left of New Colombia today is a roadside taco stand, a beach strewn with shell casings, and a small chapel containing an orange loose leaf notebook crammed full of handwritten poetry in a delicate feminine scrawl.

The thatched huts of New Colombia burned behind Trace as he walked north on the highway that afternoon. Fire trucks from Rosarita Beach and Ensenada raced to save the lonely village in flames, paying no mind to the unkempt American with a .32 revolver in his hand. Trace's Packard was in smoldering flames on the rocky beach. His suit was torn and singed but he escaped the battle without a single bullet wound. He didn't know if he would make it to the border without being arrested for murder but he had no choice but to try. He remembered that Jack Kerouac's friend Neal Cassady, legendary folk hero of the Beat movement, died this way. They found him in a coma alongside a pair of railroad tracks in Mexico in 1968, after a night of partying with booze and drugs. He was dressed only in a pair of jeans and a T-shirt and the weather that night was miserable with rain and wind. It was presumed he tried to walk into town fifteen miles away but fell asleep at some point in the journey and succumbed to the elements.

"Throw the gun away, dummy," a voice spoke at Trace's right shoulder. There was no urgency to the man's voice; in fact he seemed amused.

"Toss the gun into the rocks," the man ordered this time with urgency. "The Federales are heading this way. See the cars up ahead?"

Trace stopped at the side of the road. To his left the Pacific Ocean glittered. To his right rose the long stretch of asphalt and the golden hills where an occasional million-dollar mansion was built. His eyes felt like two heavy black orbs in his head. It was all he could do to force his eyes to focus. The man standing next to him was a bearded American, barefoot in torn jeans and a simple white cotton T-shirt. He was handsome and well built but weathered. He probably, Trace reasoned, is one of the American expatriates who live on the Baja Peninsula to escape some bad, bad things they did back home. And since Mexico has no formal extradition treaty with America, that bad thing was, invariably, homicide. But if the choice was between the Mexican police and a fellow American who probably lost his cool one night after a drinking binge and sent his wife or girlfriend screaming into the hereafter, Trace was more than willing to accept the latter.

"Follow me," the man ordered after Trace tossed the revolver into the churning ocean waves. He skittered down a rocky embankment on the beach side of the highway and rushed toward a tarpaper shack with a warning shouted over his shoulder to look out for the scorpions hiding under the rocks. Trace tried to upset not a single rock as he followed his rescuer.

"You killed Jorge Moran," the man accused Trace when they settled into the shack. It was only seven feet by seven feet with sand for a floor and a pit dug into the center for roasting fish and poultry. "Don't worry about it, man, he was strictly small fry. He didn't even track on the Mexican Mafia's radar."

"He killed Yolanda," Trace muttered.

"Who was Yolanda?" The man was rolling a joint with dirty and unsteady fingers. Outside, the scream and wail of sirens was growing more pronounced. Trace imagined that the whole village must have burned to the ground by then, including the little chapel that Moran built for Yolanda, the chapel where she married the small time thug and took her last breath on Earth.

"She was a poet I met in Silverlake."

"You're from L.A.? Cool!" The man laughed and exposed a row of broken teeth that were more likely the result of bar fights and scrapes with the Federales rather than simple neglect and decay.

Trace missed home.

Dozens of Books

"First there was the Kafka book," Trace said.

"Kafka is cool. What was that story where the guy turned into a giant bug?"

"That was *Metamorphosis*. Anyway, we're having lunch a few days later and she brings up some Chester Himes book I've never heard of and – boom! – next thing you know she drops it off for me at the front desk on her way to work the next morning."

Trace was enjoying a beer in the hotel bar and talking to his friend, the Meth Head. That's the only name Trace had for him. He was certain that the fidgety, dark-haired meth addict had provided him with a name at some point in their reckless acquaintance but Trace couldn't remember and he was too embarrassed to ask.

"I don't get where you're going with this Trace. Hey, man, if I pay you back tomorrow can you buy me a beer?"

Trace popped a handful of peanuts in his mouth and chewed slow and thoughtfully. He motioned for the bartender to set the Meth Head up with a beer and continued with his story.

"The Chester Himes book was really appealing. I mean, I devoured this thing in one day. One sitting. Blew off work to read the goddamn thing."

"Wait a minute, Hoss. You're a writer but you take a day off to read? Isn't that like a lifeguard going swimming on his day off?"

"Well, getting ahead of myself a little bit here but, yes, the point is that I did take time off to read the book. And not just that one but the next one that came in."

"What is this chick? Like chairman of the Book Of The Month Club?"

The Meth Head laughed long and loud, regurgitating tiny bubbles of beer onto the front of his filthy gray Mickey Mouse T-shirt.

"Book Of The Month? Try book of the week, book of the day. I mean, I'm dating this broad for months on end and we're going along okay. All right? I mean, no immediate sheets action because she takes thing slow in that department."

Trace took a sip of his Manhattan and then slipped his index finger into the martini glass to fish out the cherry.

"But the books," he said. "If I expressed an interest in any subject in the world, she owned a book on it. And obscure shit, too. I thought I had her beat with my Fitzgerald collection. Not just Fitzgerald's stuff but I have a shit load of critical anthologies and essays and lost stories and – well, Goddamnit, wouldn't you know she owned a book I didn't have and she sends it to me. So, after a few months we're nowhere near any kind of commitment and – "

"This is making me dizzy."

"What is? The beer or the story?"

"Both."

"I'm almost done. The point is I had dozens and dozens of her books in my place. I had to stop reading because I had so many to choose from I was getting all OCD just trying to figure out what to read."

"Come on, Trace. Is there a punch line to this story?"

"You have somewhere to go? I just bought you a beer. The punch line is this: I'm dating her for a few months, thinking that we're not moving toward anything in a committed sense of the word and then one night I finally get her back to my place – "

"Whoa, whoa, whoa, Hoss. You finally get her back to your place? After months? What is this chick, a nun? Were you dating a nun, Trace?"

Trace laughed with the Meth Head.

"No, but she was chaste in her own way. Anyway, I get her back to my place and she takes a look around and sees all of these books everywhere and she says, 'My, all of my books are here. It's like I live here already.'"

"Oh, man. That's some evil shit, Trace."

"Well, it just shows that women move in subtle ways."

"So what happened?"

Trace finished his drink and hiked his shoulders.

"I let her move in, of course."

"And?"

"She moved out six months later. And she took every fucking one of her books with her."

Cellular

"Listen to yourself, Norman. Listen to how jaded you've become."

"I'm not jaded!" Norman insisted. He was speaking from his car phone somewhere in the Santa Clarita Valley.

"You're trying to tell me that a twenty-seven-year-old porn star is old enough to play a middle-aged woman, someone's aunt no less."

"She is older," Norman persisted. "Twenty-seven is old in this business now."

"I'm not writing the role of Aunt Jesse for a twenty-seven-year-old, Norman. You've lost your mind."

"Trace, just keep repeating to yourself: it's only a porno, it's only a porno, it's only a porno. Now go smoke a bowl and write something, goddamnit."

#

"How are you doing?" Amy asked hesitantly. It was a question one always asked Trace with the slightest hesitation because it was bound to bring on a litany of complaints. She was calling from her cell phone as she drove through Brentwood.

"I'm actually doing okay," Trace replied. "I mean, I hate the shit I'm writing but I'm preaching to the choir. I know you'd much rather be working on your book than teaching or ghostwriting a tell-all memoir."

"Yes."

"All in all, I guess I'd have to say that I'm pretty lucky, huh? At least I'm still writing for a living."

"Exactly."

"Now all I have to do is convince myself of that."

Reveal the Narrator

Trace was mentoring a young writer who complained that he didn't know how to harvest from his own life experience in order to write convincing characters.

"Are you available all day today?" Trace asked one morning as he contemplated the young writer's dilemma.

His schedule was indeed open and free so they met at Trace's favorite restaurant, Foxy's in Glendale, for breakfast. When the waiter observed that Trace was walking with the aid of a cane he stepped aside with a majestic sweep of his arm and gave Trace a wide berth.

"Why do you need a cane?" the young man asked when they eased into the red vinyl booth.

"Arthritis in my hip and nerve damage in my left leg. I don't need the cane so much as I like to have it around in case something goes wrong. I have problems climbing stairs, for instance."

"Forty-eight seems awfully young to have arthritis that bad."

"Not just any arthritis. It's psoriatic arthritis brought on by severe psoriasis."

"Jeez. When did that come on?"

"A few years ago. The 'when' isn't half as important as the 'why'."

Trace ordered his usual dish, corned beef hash and eggs, and his young mentor ordered ham and eggs.

"The stress of the writing life brought on the psoriasis," Trace said as he stirred sugar and cream into his coffee. "But before that I was diagnosed as bipolar. I try to get by without meds but it's not always easy."

"My brother is manic-depressive," the writer confessed.

"Same difference. Let me ask you a question, Matt."

"Fire away." Matt poured steaming water from a steel pot over a bag of herbal tea in a coffee mug.

"What are you afraid of? What scares you the most?"

"You want me to answer that honestly?"

"As honest as you care to be," Trace said, removing the gloves that obscured his gnarled, arthritic digits. The gloves also served to hide the bright red psoriasis lesions on his hands. Matt, like everyone else, winced when he saw Trace's hands.

"I'm almost embarrassed to admit it but I'm afraid of the dark," Matt offered.

"Don't be embarrassed. A lot of people are afraid of the dark. Do you have a night light at home?"

Matt laughed. "Several. One in each room."

"I'm afraid of death," Trace admitted.

"Well, isn't that sort of a universal fear?"

"Sure it is. In 1972 I was living in Munich, Germany. Thirteen years old. My mom was married to a G.I. who was stationed there fresh out of Vietnam. He worked at the base motor pool and she worked at the base library."

Trace motioned the waiter for a coffee refill.

"Anyway, my sister and I had to have a baby-sitter – "

"You have a sister?"

"She's dead now." He sipped his coffee quietly for a moment before continuing. "We had to have a sitter, a German, to help us when we went into town or anywhere off base. Mom hired this girl, Helga, a plump little German woman, unattractive as all hell, around twenty-two years old. Helga, it appeared, was obsessed with death."

Matt leaned forward on his elbows, engrossed in Trace's words.

"Every day – sometimes she skipped a day but most every day for two weeks – Helga took my sister and I to the local funeral home that was located just at the edge of the U.S. military base in Munich. The funeral home had this vast auditorium with glassed-in walls on either side. And beyond the glass walls were the newly-dead laid out in their coffins."

"Just laid out in the open like that?"

"That's how they do it in Germany, I guess," Trace replied. "Viewings for loved ones."

"Or for anyone walking in off the streets, apparently."

"Apparently. So, Helga would take me and Lynn by the hand and walk us through the funeral home to look at all the dead laid out in their finest clothes. It was quite an experience and she was totally engrossed."

"What bothered you about it the most?"

"You ask good questions, Matt. One day there was an older German woman laid out in her coffin in a purple nightgown. It looked like sheer satin; the nightgown, I mean. And I was standing there, a thirteen-year-old boy, with my nose pushed up against the glass and this fly – this fly just landed on her nose. And I remember waiting for something, anything, a twitch of the nose, but nothing. She was really and truly dead and that was the moment I became terrified of death."

"Jesus, Trace. How long did this go on?"

"The trips to the funeral home? Two weeks. After that I ratted her out to my mother and she fired Helga on the spot after giving her a lecture about what is and isn't appropriate for children."

"How old was your sister?"

"Ten."

"Was she bothered by it, too?"

Trace hiked his shoulders. "Lynn and I rarely got along. I didn't know and I didn't really care."

After breakfast Trace suggested a trip to the beach and Matt heartily agreed to drive. It was a warm Tuesday afternoon. Trace told Matt to take Sunset Boulevard from Los Feliz all the way to Westwood and from Westwood to cut down to Santa Monica Boulevard to the pier. On the drive from Glendale to Santa Monica, Trace told Matt the story of the entire trajectory of his career, how he used assignments for porn magazines as stepping-stones to assignments for mainstream magazines, how he lucked out finding a publisher for his first novel and how that novel failed to produce the kind of success that Trace expected.

"Typical story, really," Trace said. "If you're getting into writing for the money, Matt, you're in the wrong profession."

Matt parked the car in the public lot on the Santa Monica Pier and they walked to the open-air restaurant at the end of the pier and both men ordered beers.

"The last time I was here was two years ago with Josephine."

"Your wife?"

"My ex-wife. My second ex-wife. The less said about the first one the better, except to say we produced a pretty cool kid who I rarely get to see."

Trace sipped his beer pensively.

"I was in a pretty black depression the last time Josephine and I were together. We had been separated for a while and things were looking good for a reunion and then – " Trace shrugged his shoulders. "I wrote something, a Dan Knight story – "

"I read some of those. They're very good. Let me guess: Dan Knight is your fictional alter ego."

"Yup. Well, I wrote a Dan Knight story about Jo that hurt her very much. I think I meant to hurt her to show her how much I was hurting. See, her father was dying and her mother was helpless so Jo spent the better part of a year up in the Bay Area nursing her dad to his grave while her mother looked on. It put quite a strain on our relationship."

"That's too bad."

"We rarely speak to each other. That's the real bad part. But there's an upside: between my first marriage and the marriage to Jo, I had a woman in my life – constantly at my side – for fourteen years. Now, as my career continues to hit an upswing, I'm single for the first time in that long."

"I'm only twenty-two," Matt reminded Trace. "I can't imagine being with a woman for five years, let alone fourteen."

Trace leaned on his cane. A sea breeze toyed with his blonde hair. He looked out at the Santa Monica Bay with eyes that Matt noted were a peculiar blue, an intense and electric kind of blue. At that very moment Matt could see, physically at least, why women found Trace so attractive.

"You kind of get used to having someone around. Being alone isn't always easy."

"You date though, right?"

Trace nodded. "I date. Sometimes I date too many women, to fill that void, I think."

"Anyone special?"

"Yes."

"Mind if I ask?"

"If I told you I would have to kill you."

Trace took a long swallow of his beer and lit a cigarette.

"Did you know they don't allow smoking on the beach in Santa Monica?"

"I knew that."

Trace frowned. "Fucking smoking police everywhere these days."

It was dusk by the time they hopped into Matt's Honda Civic for the long drive back to Glendale. The sky to the west was turning a shade of red mixed with soot-black.

"Brush fire," Trace muttered with all the urgency of a bowl of oatmeal. He lit a cigarette and studied the young writer as he drove. "Did you get any of this?"

"Any of what, Trace?"

"This lesson. I am mentoring you after all, right?"

"Right. Of course. I just – "

Trace frowned. "Mining what's around you for writing is as simple and easy as betraying your friends."

A sick look came across the young man's face.

"You now know my whole life," Trace said. "Go fucking write something, will you?"

All Things Must Pass

Trace missed the toilet. He jerked the soiled gray sweatpants down around his ankles but before he could make contact with the cold porcelain bowl his aggrieved stomach opened up and spilled the murky contents of his bowels all over the white linoleum floor of the hotel bathroom.

It was three o'clock in the morning. This was the third time in a week that he experienced an urgent need to rush down the hallway to the men's room in the dark hours, sometimes sidestepping a hungry mouse. No matter how many mousetraps the hotel managers set out there was always a live, prowling rodent to be found. It didn't help that the old hotel was situated above both an alleyway that was a favorite pissing spot for vagrants and a funky Italian restaurant with a questionable rating from the San Francisco Health Department.

Trace peeled off his soiled sweatpants and boxer shorts and tossed them into the green plastic waste can. He was naked except for a dirty T-shirt. He thought of jumping into the shower of the communal bathroom but the mold and mildew was more than he could stand. He dashed down the hallway to the room four doors down that he shared with Lisa. She was already stirring in bed when he returned.

"What happened?" she mumbled. Trace loomed over the bed – an aged mattress and box springs with no frame – and cleaned the excrement from his legs with a handful of fresh baby wipes. He tossed the dirty wipes into a trash bag in the corner.

"I shit myself again," Trace muttered in disgust. He pulled on his last clean pair of underwear and lit a cigarette. He sat down in the wicker armchair and stared out the window at Coit Tower in the darkness.

"You're detoxing," Lisa said, sitting up in bed with a groan.

"How can I be detoxing if I'm still drinking?" He contemptuously blew a plume of thick smoke in her direction. She pretended not to notice it was deliberate.

"You've been self-medicating like crazy ever since you went off your meds," she explained calmly and fumbled for her pack of Camel Lights on the nightstand. "You're drinking more than you're eating so your stomach is bound to be upset."

Trace went off his medications for manic depression shortly after leaving L.A. in September of 2006. He had bottomed out in Los Angeles, losing a freelancer gig with a trade magazine that catered to the adult film industry after a dispute with the executive editor over a deadline. Financial calamity ensued and Trace lost his hotel room and most of his personal belongings. The few artifacts of his life that he managed to salvage – boxes of books and his awards for writing – had been hastily shoved into a storage locker in Atwater Village before he climbed aboard the Greyhound for the long trip to San Francisco.

He had a lot of time to ponder his life during that bus trip up the coast. He didn't like most of the conclusions he came to. He could not think of himself as a failure but merely another victim of the less than charming life of a writer, a trap that many fall prey to, a thankless existence of meager royalty checks and endless pitch meetings and dull assignments for dull magazines. Peaks and valleys, highs and lows, and unexpected strings of bad luck. He was once courted by the official magazine of a major air carrier to be the

West Coast editor, but suddenly the market changed when the World Trade Center towers came tumbling down; negotiations for Trace's talents came to an abrupt halt as the magazine struggled to find its new identity.

Five years after the events of September 11, Trace found himself staring down a homeless existence in Los Angeles. That was when Lisa, an old flame, opened her doors to him in San Francisco, the city of his birth, a cold, dark, and often violent town. She lived in the Longview Hotel in the heart of North Beach. Once the notorious hangout for Beat poets and writers, North Beach was now a neighborhood of gaudy strip clubs, rowdy bars packed full of fishermen and vagrants and wanna-be poets, expensive Italian eateries, trendy coffee bistros, and dozens of low-rent residential hotels like the Longview.

Built nine years after the great quake of 1906, the Longview was once a famous bordello. Its current inhabitants were mostly down-and-outers – welfare recipients, waiters and bus boys, department store clerks, musicians, and retirees with too small a pension to afford a better place to dwell. The rooms were small – eleven feet by eleven feet – and Trace often felt trapped during the weekday afternoons when Lisa was at her job as a project manager for U.C. Berkeley across the Bay.

Days after arriving in San Francisco, Trace's depression darkened. He had stopped taking his medications because he felt they were robbing him of his creative capabilities. In less than two years he had churned out twenty-five magazine articles and seventy short stories but after the psych meds got into his system he was barely capable of writing a grocery list.

Lisa slipped him ten or twenty bucks every morning before leaving for work. He drank his breakfast at the cheapest bars he could find and usually had enough cash left over for a greasy hamburger or a grilled sausage sandwich.

By December, three months after arriving, Trace's physical and mental health was deteriorating at a rapid and alarming pace. If he could write he could find work but the muse was dead or on life support somewhere in his head. Money was scarce and they could hardly get by on Lisa's income.

"I'm forty-eight years old and I've been writing professionally for fifteen years," he complained bitterly to Lisa one evening. "It's all I know how to do and these days I can't even write a goddamn porno script. I used to be able to fall out of bed and write one of those pieces of shit."

After dinner Trace trudged down the hall to the bathroom and spilled the contents of his dinner into the toilet. This time he managed to hit the bowl. On the bathroom stall door a crude handwritten sign had been posted in response to Trace's last bowel-blowing accident:

> PLEASE DO NOT MAKE DIRTY MESS IN BATHROOM.
>
> THANK YOU. MGR.

Trace read the sign and chuckled at the rudimentary English.

"I think I have an idea for a short story," he informed Lisa when he returned from the men's room.

"Really?" She brightened.

"Yeah. It begins with a dissipated writer who dies on the toilet of a flop house hotel in San Francisco."

Maybe, he thought, I can write myself out of this goddamn mess after all.

Epilogue
Return To New Colombia

"So, I read the Trace Mexico story."

"And?"

"It was interesting. Experimental and surreal, very creative."

"Do you think it works as a stand-alone piece? I mean, a village burns down and Trace kills people and nothing is explained."

"Trace *allegedly* kills people. You never came right out and said he killed anyone."

"True. But there is a whole backstory to that story. I wrote what I did in one fast, manic blast and then sat on the story for three days, trying to figure out how to write the rest of it. Finally, I just said 'Fuck it' and published it as is. I like it."

"What's the backstory?"

"Well – " Rodger lit a cigarette and took a sip of his beer. "Trace goes on a dare issued by Amy, sort of a scavenger hunt."

"Amy being your married writer friend."

"*Trace's* married writer friend. You know that full well. Why did you feel the need to interject that?"

"Just to keep your readers up to speed."

"Oh. Okay. So, she's out of town for two weeks doing a rewrite on a movie."

"Amy is out of town."

"Correct. And before she leaves she issues Trace a challenge: find a poetess and fall in love or, at least, fall in lust. So Trace starts haunting all these funky book shops and poetry readings in Silverlake and Echo Park and he's really quite nauseated by all the pretense going on and everything."

"Trace among pretentious poets," Shirley said with a hearty laugh. "That's a good one."

"Before I go too far, I should mention that the original title was *A Million Dollar Sunset*; that's important to know as it factors into the ending with the burning village and all."

Shirley curled one slender leg under her hip on the bed in their hotel room.

"Anyway, he finds this poetess at a reading in Silverlake. To cut to the chase, they fall in love but she has some shadowy shit going on, namely a husband in Mexico who is a small time drug dealer and local thug in this small village called New Colombia."

"Does New Colombia actually exist?"

"No, totally fiction. She ends up going back to New Colombia and Trace follows her and a confrontation ensues between Trace and the husband. The poetess has fallen in love with Trace and wants to return to L.A. with him but the husband, Jorge, will hear nothing of it. Jorge offers Trace one million dollars to return his wife to him and Trace says, 'I can't make your wife love you again for a million dollars. You can't have her back.' And then a gunfight ensues and that's where the story I'm writing picks up, after the gunfight."

"So the poetess is killed?"

"Murdered by the husband. In this little wedding chapel he built for them in the middle of town. Trace finds her notebook of original poetry on the chapel altar and that's when he freaks out, grabs a gun and – aw, you see how complicated it got? There's no wonder I didn't feel like writing the whole damn thing."

"Any other reasons?"

"Yeah, I started it during a manic episode. I didn't think I was supposed to get those while on psych meds."

THE END

About the Author

RODGER JACOBS has won multiple awards and grants for his work as a journalist, documentary writer and producer, screenwriter, playwright, magazine editor, true crime writer, book critic and columnist for *PopMatters*, and live event producer. He provided the preface and original inspiration for *Jack London: San Francisco Stories* (Sydney Samizdat Press) in 2010.